ANNA JANE VARDILL

THE SECRETS OF CABALISM

THIS IS A SNUGGLY BOOK

ISBN: 978-1-64525-135-4

THE SECRETS OF CABALISM

Anna Jane Vardill (1781-1852) was born in London, the daughter of the American-born pamphleteer, poet and spy John Vardill, who familiarized her with the poets of antiquity. Her first published work was *Poems and Translations* (1809), which was followed by *The Pleasures of Human Life* (1812). Using the signature "V." she published a large body of work in *The European Magazine*, many pieces of which have been, over the years, reprinted and translated, usually without offering her credit or, worse still, attributing the pieces to other authors.

SNUGGLY BOOKS

CONTENTS

A NOTE ON THE TEXTS

THE current volume reproduces six texts which, under the heading "The Secrets of Cabalism," and bearing the signature "V.," were published from January 1821 to June 1821 in *The European Magazine*. The texts are presented for the most part as they originally appeared, though some obvious errors have been corrected, and a few spellings regularized and modernized.

Several of the items here have been reprinted in various places, often uncredited or misattributed, and sometimes with various textual differences. The most noteworthy of these reprints is likely that in *Great British Tales of Terror: Gothic Stories of Horror and Romance 1765–1840*, edited by Peter Haining, in which he reproduces chapter IV of the present volume and attributes it, without offering any evidence or rationale, to William Child Green, an error which was carried forward through five editions, including four by Penguin Books, as well as another similar edition under another title.

THE
SECRETS
OF
CABALISM

I

THE account given of the Cabalists in an extract from "Le Compte de Gabalis," renders much detail of their principles unnecessary. But the beautiful dream of Rosicrucius was mingled in the last century with more dangerous fanaticism. After fabling elegantly with gnomes, sylphs, nymphs and salamanders, a few philosophers amused themselves with a creed, by which they compounded human nature of the four elements, and ascribed the vivacity, meekness, fortitude, or apathy of the soul, to the prevalence of one or more of these constituents. It was not difficult to graft a kind of fatalism on this creed; for if the actions of men are caused by the influence of a prevailing element, they are in some degree predestined to such actions and not morally responsible. The next inference is, that such combinations of the four great principles of life, fire, water, earth, and air, must be accidental, or subject to no ruling providence. Thus, at least, a few German metaphysicians reasoned, and their disciples were very well pleased with a system so accommodating.

In the last years of Gustavus the Third's reign, when the French revolution had thrown upwards all the froth of modern philosophy, a sect of this kind found its way into Gothland. One of its proselytes was a descendant of the great Wallenstein, and father of a young captain in the royal guard, whose misconduct caused one of its companies to be disbanded, and their officers expelled from Sweden. Count Wallenstein heard of his son's disgrace with considerable coldness. "There is too much of the fluctuating and uncertain element in that boy," said the cabalistical father;—"some fountain-nymph, some blue-eyed Egeria, will find employment for a Numa so young and romantic. I shall leave him to seek a guardian in his own element."

After this speech Count Wallenstein named his son no more, and seemed to bury himself in his new studies. He employed a French mechanic to construct for him an automaton of great power, capable, when the stone to which it was attached received any pressure, of advancing, rising and moving its hands with significant and inviting gestures. He was heard to say, on the authority of some profound students, that mechanism and chemistry might go near to produce a human being, and his labours to perfect his favourite work were very long and private. Whether he hoped to animate it like a second Prometheus, and what means he pursued, were known only to himself and his confidential artisan.—Secrecy has always been an essential part of cabalism, and perhaps not the least charm to its professors.

There was at some distance from the little river Wreda, a low wooden house occupied by an unknown Frenchman. He had neither wife nor child, nor any servant except a negress, whose shape and colour were amply sufficient to dismay intrusive spies. The Swedish peasants had no hesitation in pronouncing her one of those sorceresses whose incantations are still feared, yet permitted, in the North. The habitation of these two recluses was in the hollow of a defile made by two rocks, whose faces so nearly met, that the sun could seldom penetrate to their utmost depth even in his highest noon. These rocks were desolately bare, except when the thin white smoke from Bertrand's chimney rose curling over their sides, and gave a kind of softness to their

purple tint. Two goats and a watch-dog occupied the narrow stockade or enclosure which
the Frenchman and his negress had erected
round their dwelling, into which no guest
was ever admitted. They had spent seventeen
years in its seclusion, but Bertrand was not
always within his own walls. He took weekly
and sometimes daily walks of great length,
and his faithful Mooma was not permitted
to enquire into their purpose. They might be
to make purchases at the next hamlet, for he
generally carried with him a knapsack or large
basket, and in the beginning of the winter
he was more inquisitive respecting shamoy
and furs than appeared necessary for his own
wardrobe. But the eighteenth winter brought
with it a fatal disease which prevented his
excursions, and he looked every day at the
setting sun, or at the rings which marked the
progress of time on his pine-tree torch, with
frantic impatience. When three weeks of the
darkest month had passed, Bertrand called
Mooma to the side of his mattrass, pointed to
a basket which stood empty beside him, and
commanded her to fill it with some cakes of
rye-flour, a flask of milk, and a piece of hon-
eycomb which he had selected. He beckoned
to the dog which usually attended his walks,
and seemed as if he had been going to add

some urgent orders, but the hand of death was on him. He stretched his hand towards the door with a cry of agony, and died.

Mooma's intellect was well suited to the degree of abject servitude she had borne so many years. To obey her master, to prepare his coarse food, and perform the drudgery of his hovel, was all her knowledge, and she had been content to share his kindness with the animals domesticated about her. She looked at Bertrand's stiffening features with very little comprehension of the dismal change his death might produce in her situation; and when she had composed his body, and sung the wild melody of an African dirge, she took up the basket and set forth, guided by the unchanging instinct of obedience.

The huge watch-dog seemed to hesitate between his desire to remain with his dead master and his accustomed duty of attending the basket. The latter prevailed, and Mooma following his gambols as he snuffed his way through the drifted snow, arrived, after a very long walk, at a place which seemed to her superstitious eyes a mansion for some unknown deity. It was a large circular space about half a mile in extent, covered with smooth and shining ice, except in the centre, where a tuft of dwarf trees crusted with icicles appeared

like a knot of crystal pillars wreathed with diamonds. Something like a dim haze hovered
over the highest, and sometimes floated in the
wind, while Mooma stood gazing on it as if it
had been the breathing of the deity she feared.
Her shaggy companion shewed less fear, and
seizing the basket from her hand, walked
across the blue circle of ice, and deposited it
among the frozen trees. He returned bound-
ing and gambolling, till Mooma, conceiving
that this offering of food was meant by her
dead master to propitiate some unseen power,
such as her savage countrymen worshipped,
turned her face homewards, hoping to have
secured the happy passage of his soul.

Bertrand lay undisturbed in his
winding-sheet when she returned to his hut;
and this faithful servant's next task was to
deposit him under the richest turf in his little
garden. She decorated it with a few beads and
shells, all that she had preserved of her native
land, and sang the dirge of her tribe, until the
bitterness of the midnight frost forced her
back to her solitary hearth. Winter passed and
spring returned without causing any change
in her mode of life, for her little stock of oil,
rye-flour, and the milk of her goats, sufficed for
light and nourishment. And the dog's gestures
and joyful bark reminded her every seventh

morning to replenish the basket, and carry it again to the spot which seemed familiar to him: and Mooma still believing this a religious rite in some way useful to her dead master, fulfilled it with humble and patient fidelity.

But as the brighter and warmer days approached, the scene of her mysterious duty changed from a sheet of ice to a lovely lake, and the bower in the centre became green. Still the dog plunged resolutely with his charge into the water, swam across, and having deposited it in some invisible recess, returned with his usual expressions of delight. And in this dreary and unfrequented region, the poor negress found comfort in these excursions to perform what seemed a communion with some friendly spirit of the water.

Curiosity has so little part in the uncultivated African's character, that Mooma might have continued her obedience to Bertrand's last command without further investigation, and with a comforting belief that her little tenement's safety was secured by this mysterious ceremony. But on the 19th of March 1792, as she returned from her weekly excursion, her dog's furious howlings and the print of strange feet in the snow informed her of a stranger's visit. Opening the door of her hut, and looking round, she saw the coffer of her dead master had been ransacked, and the only apparel it contained taken out. Part of a rye-loaf and a flask of rum had been taken also, but a small piece of silver was left on the board. It appeared to Mooma of so much more value than the things removed, that she fell on her knees and kissed it with reverence, as the gift of that beneficent spirit to which she paid, as she supposed, her weekly tributes. In one respect Mooma was not mistaken. The rixdollar was in reality much more in worth than the tattered grey cloak and suit of shamoy leather which the interloper had purloined, but they were of infinite value in his eyes, and except the morsel of rye-bread moistened in rum, he had tasted nothing for several hours. Clothed in his stolen garb, he made haste to a lonely road which led by many detours and dangerous precipices to a house near the town called Granna.

This house was large, and had the air of a nobleman's mansion, though ill-built and neglected. Our stranger forced himself through a broken gate into a green courtyard, and through a loophole once meant for an arrow-slit into the interior of this house, where no one seemed likely to oppose him: for only an old man was sitting alone in a sort of laboratory; and the figure of the intruder so much resembled the great Tycho Brahe's in his grotesque fur-cap and ill-suited leathern coat, that the student stood aghast as if his lucubrations had raised the ghost of Danish philosophy.

"Put out the lights," said the newcomer sternly—"the seventeenth of March is over—he is dead——"

Count Wallenstein knew his son's voice, and ran to embrace him—"I have not an hour to lose," added young Otto—"the gates of the city are shut—I escaped thus far by miracle—are you alone?"

"What is done! what is escaped!" asked the old Count, as if he had feared to understand the desperate import of his son's countenance. Otto made no answer, and the trampling of horses towards his house announced the extremity of danger. "Take this ring and this purse, my son—pass through the lowest window, and keep to the right of the lake—if no smoke is rising, wait till a woman's hand beckons among the rocks."

Young Wallenstein made but one leap through the outlet into his father's deserted park, and heard the clanging of horses' hoofs before the gate as their riders drew themselves round in array to prevent the flight of any inhabitant. But he had strong nerves and muscles—every winding was known to him, and he crept under and among piles of drifted snow, which the early sun of spring had not yet dissolved. He was soon out of sight and hearing—the immediate danger was passed, and he went at a tardier pace to the lake. What place of refuge was he to expect there! Every thing on its banks was silent and desolate, but perhaps the absence of all human visitants might be his father's motive for selecting such an asylum. But as he listened with ears quickened by alarm, the word of command given to soldiers, whose trumpet sounded dully on the frozen air, was distinctly audible. There was no alternative: a pile of rocks seemed at a safe distance near the centre; and before the first horseman had turned upon the banks, Otto plunged in, and swam desperately towards it.

Meanwhile Count Wallenstein received the visit of an armed detachment with the courtesy and coolness of an accomplished statesman. He permitted their official search, heard their strange intelligence, which the commander hardly ventured to hint, and dismissed them with abundant promises to assist their purpose. When the troop had left his domain, he sent his few servants to their beds, and retired himself to his laboratory. He sat there musing and in deep silence till he supposed all asleep.

Then with his lamp in one hand and a mask in the other, he descended to the lowest apartment of his house. He was followed unseen by an armed man, the commander of the troop which had visited him to search his tenement a few hours before. This man knew the strange and reserved character of Count Wallenstein, and, by bribing a menial, had obtained means of re-entering and watching. He was not disappointed in his expectations of discovering something. Through the crevice of a door studded with iron, but shrunk by age, he saw eleven men seated round a table lighted by the single lamp which the elder Wallenstein had placed upon it.

"We are all assembled," said one at the head of the assembly, "except one—yet the seventeenth of March is past."

"Past, but seen only through a shadow," answered another voice—"we know not yet how far the spirits of earth may subdue those of a nobler element."

"If to give earth to earth be a deed fit for those who profess to be nowise akin to earthly things," replied the first speaker, bending down his head and crossing his arms on the horoscope spread before him.—"Had this thing prospered," he added, in a broken tone, "the twelfth chair at this table would not have been vacant now. We have trusted too much to our wisdom—too little to Providence."

"To Providence," was echoed by a dark gaunt man, whose face, though half masked, discovered the grimness of a maniac—"What is that Providence?—If, as our great master teaches us, the elements have separate ministers that busy themselves in the affairs of men, there is not one but many providences, and we have no right to doubt that one of them at least will befriend us."

"You are right," said Wallenstein—"And why should a word affright us?—What ignorant men call death is but the transmigration of a spirit to its parent element. He who fell on Tuesday had a soul which the world said was a spark of the rarest fire—What if he has passed by the help of fire into a better and fitter state?"

"Still," answered the first speaker, "I see not how we had a right to dispossess his body of that spark by force. If the elements were not blended in him so justly as our science deems fit, we have yet no right to dissolve what we could not amend."

"We have not dissolved, we have only altered," interrupted the enthusiast fiercely—"Earth will receive her part of him—fire has claimed its own—air has his last breath—

water—O! there was nothing of that pure and gentle element in his composition. But," he added, pausing and looking at the former speaker, "enough of its coldest particles are in some among us."

"There is iron in water," retorted his opponent, "and you may find strength where there seems only temperance. If the spirits of the element you name delight in murder, it would have been well if they had all been smothered when the upper crust of the earth fell in, as your philosophers pretend, at the first deluge."

The sarcastic sneer on his lip, betrayed by the curl of his thick mustachio, was not unobserved by Wallenstein, who filled his huge silver cup to the brim. "Whatever be the power and properties of water," he said, in a jovial tone, "we will not try them here. Brothers and friends, let us drink to the nymph of the Wreden lake."

The masked Divan rose, pledged the cup with joined hands, and their president instantly extinguished the lamp. It seemed as if they all departed by different doors, and the Swedish soldier was left alone in his covert. He was powerfully and strangely affected by all he had seen. The mysticism of their language, the apparatus of crucibles and Leyden jars, and the bags of earth, stoves, and bladders, attached to the persons of the speakers, appeared at once grotesque and hideous. There was enough, however, to excite both his curiosity and his loyal zeal, and the last allusion to the Wreden lake determined him to adventure there. He left the house by the same means that had enabled him to enter it, and bent his steps to the banks which his troop had already reconnoitred. The Swede mused all the way on the obscure hints he had gathered concerning the spirits of the water, and paused once or twice before he tried his strength in swimming across the lake to the island-rock where he supposed the murderer might be concealed. By frequent and cautious surveys, he discovered a prominent rock in a part of the islet nearest the main shore, distinguished by something like a flight of steps. He even imagined, as the water lay calm and clear, that the fragments of rock piled under these steps had the appearance of an artificial barricade. The soldier's eye was keen and experienced. He dived like a bird of the water, and alighted on a point very little below its surface. But an apparition rose before him which seemed to change his blood into the same cold element. A creature gradually advanced from behind the reef of caverned rocks in the semblance of a female. Her long dripping hair was tangled with weeds and sand, but there was motion in her eyes and in the hands that seemed to act like oars upon the water. Presently, she rose breast-high above it, and remained still, her neck shining in the moonlight like polished ivory. The soldier's eyes fastened themselves on this spectacle, and all that he had heard of the Count's communion with beings of another species came upon his thoughts. Still he stood firm on the base of the rock, though without strength enough to move. The mer-maiden, if such a name may be given to the nymph of the lake, only raised her hand as if to beckon him away, and her large blue eyes dwelt on him with a fascinating gaze. Either his dazzled eyes or the motion of the water seemed to bring her nearer; and making one instinctive effort, he charged his carbine which he had brought slung over his shoulder, and fired. The ball rebounded as from a stone, but the flash of another musquet passed close to his head. The soldier, however daunted by a nymph of the lake, had no fears of ordinary beings, and deeming he had a mortal enemy to deal with, he stepped back, and again loading his fusil, discharged it through the crevice from whence the hostile bullet had proceeded. It was answered by a deadly groan. He bent down, and looking into the chasm, saw Count Wallenstein's son struggling with death. The generous soldier raised him up, and would have forced a cordial into his lips. "It is too late," said Otto, "but I have lived long enough. Carry me farther into the cave, and let me die."

"Ah, Wallenstein!" said the soldier, "why did you not trust me?—How could I expect to find you in this deplorable disguise? But the seventeenth of March is past, and the King still lives."

"He must die!" answered Otto; "Ankerstroem charged his pistol trebly, and his aim was sure. Make your own escape. There is a peril nearer than you dream of!"

He would have said more, but voice and life failed him. His last words only roused and confirmed the courage of the Swedish soldier. He took the cap and cloak of the dead body, and went further into the cave, from which a thin smoke seemed to ascend. It guided him to a kind of recess arched with the living rock, and lighted only by a fire of pine-tree. Near it sat a man of singularly gaunt and grim figure muffled in a military cloak, with a large sack beside him.—"Make your escape," said the soldier, imitating the voice and phrase of young Wallenstein—"there is a peril nearer than you dream of."—"What then?" retorted the ruffian—"have I not shared it with our comrades eighteen months—Thanks to the faithful fool, and a dog's cunning, we have not starved here. What! did the wooden mermaid scare away the spy?"—"He is safe," said the loyal Swede, lowering his voice, and retiring into the most shadowy corner.—"So will I be!" rejoined his companion—"Your master Rosicrucius had an iron effigy to guard his tomb—his disciples have a painted one to secure their treasury—I will shew you better machinery." So saying, he made a leap towards the outlet of the cave, but the troop had forded the lake and crowded in to the assistance of their commander. They seized the regicide's accomplice, and found in the recesses of the cave all the correspondence, gold, weapons, and ammunition of the traitorous cabal. The automaton artfully constructed to guard the entrance when the foot of a stranger invaded it, was hewn to pieces, and Ankerstroem's miserable death on the scaffold terminated one daring effort of political cabalism.

II

"NO," said the prime-minister of Christian VII, as he sat in the confidential cabinet of his colleague, Count Brandt—"that is too much for any human capacity of belief. I can see our master's imbecility of head and hardness of heart, but I cannot believe him a composition of plumbago, or black lead."

"You should rather say that you believe him a lump of silex, for black lead has too much affinity to the diamond to have afforded him either head or heart. But, Struensee!—are you, versed in all the monstrous superstitions of Asia, Africa, and ancient Europe, prepared to say my system is incredible?—What is there more unnatural in believing all the elements which surround us inhabited by active and intelligent beings, than in peopling them with the profligate and hideous deities of heathen and Hindoo mythology?"

"We now understand the Sublime allegory of both without believing either; and I frankly add, that I have studied the wild yet elegant romance of Rosicrucius not so much to enrich my mind as to relieve it by ideas of moral beauty, which are not supplied by realities."

"That is," said the designing philosopher, "you have formed a *beau ideal*. Tell me, while we are in the secret safety of this cabinet, with what part of human nature you could best dispense?—With its infirmities, of course?"

"I wish," replied the young statesman, rising with energy, "that we had stronger reason, or no feelings. Brandt, all that yet has happened in my public life, convinces me we should be always wise, and therefore always easy, if we had none. Of what use is our indignation at dishonesty?—there are always a thousand reasons why it is not safe to express it.—We are required to submit patiently and daily to injustice, and our vivid sense of it is only a torment. Is there any feeling of joy, of friendship, or of triumph, which we are not forced to curb and suspect? Let me find, if I can, a creature framed for reason only, and I shall expect to see perfection."

Brandt smiled at this sally, and at the high flush of excited feeling which coloured the speaker's countenance. "You have said enough,

Struensee, to shew me what materials I must choose for your gratification, and to convince your unbelief." So saying, he unlocked an iron coffer, and placed on the table two fragments of stone.

"This," continued the cabalist, "is a part of that immense stone which eastern nations call Saxhrat, and believe the centre or axis of the earth. It was dislodged in one of those earthquakes which they suppose the Creator produces by commanding this stone to move one of its vast fibres. This smaller fragment came from that great tract northwards of Mexico, named Anahuas, and rich in ores and precious stones of every kind. The first contains portions of the six primitive rocks:—granite, porphyry, marble, serpentine, schist, and sienite;—the second includes the principies of all the oriental gems, the topaz, the emerald, the ruby, and the sapphire. Among the sullen and unpromising materials of the rocky fragment, I can find the occidental gems, the cornelian, sardonyx, agate, opal, mocha, jasper, and garnet. And into one or all of these I can convey life by certain combinations. There are beings who inhabit and govern these masses—choose whether you desire to know them better, for they partake the nature of the substance they rule."

Struensee smiled incredulously, and replied—"If I desired a superhuman wife, I would choose one, like Mahomet's angels, composed of seven kinds of incense, rather than one derived from clay or rock, however modified into gems. But if you ask what gem I should desire to animate, I would choose the diamond, which lightning cannot penetrate, nor the utmost violence deprive of its qualities, I choose it because its hardness, its brightness, and incorruptible nature, realize my notion of a mind all truth and justice without that beautiful defect called feeling."

"You are mistaken, however," said his companion;—"and the diamond unites some properties very foreign to your notion; for though it affords no ashes when exposed to fire, it ends in the most poisonous vapour. And the charcoal and oxygen which compose it are too obstinate and volatile to complete your poetical comparison. But we will see what chemic art can produce under a Rosicrucian's guidance."

Brandt opened what has since been called a Voltaic apparatus; and after sundry experiments aided by enormous heat, fused a small lump of charcoal, to which he added a most minute portion of oxygen.[1] The result was, or

1 It would be well if this Danish statesman had be-

seemed to be, a diamond of rare lustre, and such breadth of surface, that it resembled the crystal which covered a small portrait. And when Struensee looked upon it, a miniature face of exquisite colouring and beauty appeared within it, varying as the light glanced on the gem which contained it, as if it had life and motion. The young statesman was confounded at this specimen of cabalistic art, and especially as the visionary face was one he had imagined in his dreams of beauty. "You are surprised," said Brandt, "at my discernment and my skill. You have not yet seen the sequel. Keep this gem—its power depends on the wearer's affinity to the principles it possesses. Strength, firmness, and integrity, are the moral qualities which resemble the diamond—it has no fallibility, no soft particle, no power of change. Remember and preserve it."

The cabalist fixed his eyes sternly on Struensee, who understood the admonition. They were both engaged in plans, perhaps too romantic, for the reformation of Danish policy; and the weakness of the sovereign, while it permitted daring attempts, increased the hazard of those who had no support

---

queathed his secret; for no heat has yet been found sufficient to fuse charcoal by the most celebrated modern chemists.

except their own talents. Brandt knew how much truth and honour were mingled with the enthusiasm of Struensee's character, and also knew how far the charm of mystery acts on the firmest human nature. Artfully descending from the pomp of his philosophic harangue, he led his young colleague back to the secret of state-policy which had caused their meeting, and sketched the extensive plot a few days was to unfold.

On the third day from this cabalistic conference, the young queen Caroline-Matilda was expected to preside at a dramatic entertainment, composed, in compliment to her native country, in the English language. Count Brandt had given the half-idiot king a sufficient taste for necromantic wonders, and in due compliance with his taste, the drama was founded on the agency of a sylph, attached to a learned and discontented man. This latter character fell to the lot of Count Struensee, who studied it with zeal and delight, because it really suited the romantic bent of his genius, and his gallant readiness to amuse an amiable and ill-matched stranger; the part of the sylph was sustained by a creature attired in the lightest drapery, but impenetrably veiled. The King seemed enchanted with her gestures and her voice, especially, perhaps, because no one could inform him from whence the actress came. His own inability to penetrate any thing obscure, and the delight which folly always finds in mysteries, increased the charm of the incognita. He was standing in a stupid but very happy trance of wonder, when Count Brandt presented himself. "Your questions and conjectures, sire," said the accomplished cabalist, "are all misapplied. Whoever has presumed to guess who or what the stranger really is, has no right to be believed. She is the creation of my art, and I have fulfilled my promise to your Majesty."

The king, in a still higher humour of joy, required him to call her back and reveal her name.

"She has no name, unless, sire, you are pleased to called her Adama, or the Diamond. But she shall appear again at your command, with a dramatis personæ of her own species."

"But," interposed the King, "let her dispense with that ungraceful and unfriendly veil."

"Her veil," answered Brandt, "is the woven amianthus, and partakes of the fossil kind from which some of her kindred beings spring." —Then shewing two small caskets of ebony, and ivory, containing, as he said, the oriental and occidental earths, he desired the king to make his choice. Christian chose the oriental, and Brandt, opening his ivory box, scattered a little earth upon the table, muttering the celebrated cabalistical word "Ετημλογηχομυςτιχος."

At this moment a delicious symphony, produced by the invention of an ingenious chemist on wires and bells governed by electric fluid, astonished some part of the audience; and the king, seated between Brandt and Struensee, saw a groupe of exquisite figures suddenly emerge from beneath the canopy. One wore a veil of pale blue, another of the softest green; the third and fourth had garments which seemed dipped in the dye of the topaz and the ruby, but the fifth wore a mantle that appeared, from its singular lustre and transparency, to be composed of filaments of spunglass, so flexible yet so bright were the foldings of the tissue. As these lovely figures wreathed themselves in their dance, they resembled flowers arranged in a well-chosen garland; and the king, powerfully affected with surprise and a sense of that kind of beauty which promises pleasure, asked Brandt if these were substances or shadows.

"Your Majesty sees," he answered, "the spirits of those gems which spring from mere alumine or clay—a substance the most stubborn in the world, yet its offsprings are brittle, brilliant, and pellucid. They have life and motion, but passions are unknown to them,—in this, at least, they resemble their parent."

"For what purpose, then," interrupted Christian, "have they any existence?"

"They are visible only to those whose actions require judgment and fortitude. Princes and legislators have a right to their presence, but they can behold them only while their minds are occupied, as your Majesty's now is, in philosophic investigation, or in beneficent projects, such as have been suggested to you for the enfranchisement of your poor subjects."

The king paused earnestly with a serious gaze; and turning to Struensee, said—"Who is she that stands in the centre?—It is the shape and stature of my wife."

"Your Majesty sees with the eye of a young husband,—the spirit of the diamond has no fixed complexion, and whoever is permitted to discern her always imagines that she resembles what he prizes best. Look again, and you will find in her face all the beauty that creates love."

"Ah!" said Christian, with the sudden light of intellect which sometimes breaks on idiotism, "that is the only true beauty,—but I see the face of Caroline-Matilda of England, not of my own Dina."

The figure on which the king gazed instantly dropped her shining veil, and wrapped herself in one, whose whiteness resembled that of the swan's down, but it concealed her features entirely. "I have told you," said Brandt, "the nature of these Gnomes. Still possessed of the properties of earth, they are incapable of social enjoyment, and cannot administer to ours. The fire that passed through your Majesty's fancy,—the feelings of youthful affection that revived as you spoke of a former favourite, have disturbed the sober and cold frame of mind requisite to discern these preternatural beings. Ah, Sire! their beauty cannot be wholly unfolded to you till you have completed that great effort which will prove and establish the independence of your spirit."—As the cabalist spoke, a sudden darkness covered the saloon; and when it vanished, nothing remained of the beautiful vision, except a leaf of laurel on which a diamond hung like a dew-drop, at the king's feet.

During the whole of this dialogue, Struensee had no eyes, except for the beautiful dancer who had worn the veil of remarkable whiteness without transparency. It had answered completely the purpose of a mask, but her person so resembled the Queen Matilda's, that Struensee felt a kind of remorse mingling with the pleasure which her presence excited. That pleasure had not been invisible or unobserved. Count Moltke, the favourite confidante of the dowager-queen, had been placed among the audience to watch his conduct, and executed his office with the bitter zeal of a displaced minister and an ambitious woman's agent. Cowering among the trees that formed an avenue from the illuminated theatre to the queen's ballroom, he expected to see her pass without her veil, that he might identify her with the unknown actress, and fixed the suspicions he had already roused in her duped husband. But he only saw the king leaning familiarly on the arm of Count Brandt, who led him into one of the lighted temples which the queen's taste had erected in her gardens. He followed secretly and closely, till he saw them seated at a table on which Brandt spread a paper, and pointed to a place for the king's signature. "Sire;" he heard him say, "you designed this night only to gratify philosophic curiosity,—you will render it an era in moral and political regeneration if you sign this decree. You have seen the secrets of Nature revealed by my humble means; recompense her for the discovery by liberating and enlightening her sons. I have made you acquainted with a being sprung only from the basest element, from mere impenetrable clay,—deign, sire, to acquaint yourself with your fellow-creatures,—your countrymen, your subjects, by elevating them from bondage, and giving them a portion of freedom and instruction. If that intelligent and fair creature came at my command to-night, what may not spring from your influence over the noblest race of men?"

The king cast his eyes, in which the hazy light of intoxication was visible, on a shaded recess between the pillars. Moltke himself was surprised to see the figure of the sylph-actress standing as if covered with a veil of transparent diamond. Christian rose to catch her, but some impenetrable substance seemed to resist his touch. "A Rosicrucian knows," said the cabalist, "that the spirits of the elements can be approached only by those who resemble them. Your Majesty has not yet shewn the firmness of the gem in which that lovely spirit is embodied. There is only one act wanting to prove it."

Christian put his agitated hand to the official paper, and signed it almost illegibly; and Struensee, who entered almost at the same instant, exchanged a glance with his colleague which congratulated him on his success. But the veiled figure disappeared as he presented himself; and while their eyes and their credulous master's dwelt upon the space she had left, they did not perceive the hand that removed the paper from the table. When they looked round towards each other, they had no suspicion that another had been substituted. Count Brandt placed the false paper carefully in his portfolio, and returned with his sovereign and Struensee to join the gala. Moltke, stealing from his hiding-place, made haste to seek the queen-dowager, and shewed her an order for the arrest of Caroline-Matilda, signed by the king's hand.

"This shall be executed to-night," said the crafty statesman—"and Brandt has in his portfolio an absolute warrant to detain Struensee in close custody. Stupid contrivers!—while they performed their burlesque phantasmagoria to amuse your son, their precious act for the advancement of the peasantry was exchanged for one of more immediate benefit. And the best part of the machinery is, that each of these reforming ministers will think himself duped by the other. Thus we shall break both their alliance and their project."

Before the daybreak Caroline-Matilda was conveyed to prison with her infant son; and Brandt had unwarily delivered his portfolio into the hands of his secretary, a spy purchased by his enemy. This perfidious colleague instantly conveyed it to Count Moltke, who assembled proper officers, and, accompanied by his agent, entered Struensee's bed-chamber, and arrested him. At the sight of his friend's secretary, and of that paper which he had seen signed with such high hopes, the certainty of most deep fraud smote him. Count Moltke was not slow in enforcing the stroke. "You are charged," said he, "on evident proofs, of undue favour from the queen, and I am an eye-witness of your sinister attempts to distract the king by exhibitions of art-magic and cabalism. Give me that jewel which an infatuated woman has lavished on you from her husband's regalia, and thank my kindness for removing from your person a testimonial so decisive of your guilt."

Struensee was compelled to surrender the diamond with a powerful feeling of disgust and indignation at the stratagem employed by Brandt to fix on him the strongest appearances of treason. And while they lodged him in that state-prison which he knew he should never leave, except to perish on the scaffold, he exectrated and renounced the philanthropy whose excess had tempted him to serve his countrymen and trust his colleague at the hazard of life and honour.

The day appointed for his execution came, and the tolling of a bell indicated the hour. It was scarcely dawn. By a dull lantern-light he was led into the yard of his prison, and put into a coach strongly guarded. His journey, he expected, would terminate at the public place of execution, and he was surprised to see the coach turn through the city-gates into a lonely road. It stopped at the frontiers, and the commandant of his escort alighted, and entered with him into a miserable hut called a post-house. "Struensee—you are free—under your name, and in your attire, another state-prisoner was executed this morning at Copenhagen. Take back this diamond, and do not ask me by what means it is restored to you as the means of your future fortune. Keep the seal of this packet unbroken seven years, and let its contents be known only to yourself."

Struensee was thunderstruck, and hardly sensible of joy at this dismission. His ambition, his benevolence, even his capacity for friendship, were all destroyed by the deadly plot of which he had been the victim. But he was still young, rich in a jewel of immense value, conscious of innocence, and apparently secure from his public enemies. He retired to a small farm which he possessed in Silesia, and lived under an assumed name, entirely estranged from the world. If he could have re-gained those warm and active feelings which disappointment had crushed, he might have been useful and happy. Nothing, however, could recall the trusting, hoping, and cheerful spirit of his youth. He had seen the woman he thought loveliest debased by artifice; his friend had betrayed him, and the people for whom he would have hazarded life and great-ness joined in the vilest libels[1] on his memory. But as the dryness and desolation of his heart encreased, he became timid and avaricious, and hoarded the diamond with anxious care. He was not less tenacious of the secret packet; and when seven years had worn away, he found its contents in the hand-writing of Count Brandt, and in these few words:—

April 27th, 1772.

I shall expiate my political rashness to-morrow on the scaf-fold, and the queen's connivance in our dangerous drama will cost her liberty, perhaps her life. But I have done enough. I promised to make you acquainted with that

---

1 "Malum STRUENS SE ipsum perdidit," was the motto usually annexed to Struensee's portrait by his enemies.

preternatural thing,—a creature capable of reason, but destitute of all human or social feeling, —in other words, capable of no affection, no hope, and no effort. I am told your demeanour in the prison was that of sullen and determined apathy, which, if I understand your character, will soon transform you to the thing you desired to see. I told you truly,—the diamond has no power except over those who resemble its hard and impenetrable nature. If the spirit which has entered your mind has debased you to a level with coarse earth, the gems it composes will be all you are now capable of valuing. Keep this as my legacy, and one of the *Secrets of Cabalism*.

III

IT has been matter of much marvel among casuists why countries far remote, and men wholly unlike in habits and constitution, should have the same superstitions and pastimes:—yet as human nature is every where alike in general, there is no more wonder that its follies should be similar than that trees of the same species should put forth nearly the same kind of blossoms in all climates, though the size and colouring may differ according to the richness of the soil. About the year 1770, a Dutch merchant named Donderdonk settled at New York, and became remarkable alike for the amplitude of his purse and person. Though the Dutch settlers in that colony had very little reverence for poetic fables, they carried with them and cherished all the legends of St. Nicholas, and paid great attention to a custom supposed to have been brought from the ancient isle of Cytherea, authorizing the girls to beat all the boys who ventured abroad on the first of April, and on the second of that month to receive a counter flagellation from any male urchin whose courage was equal to reprisal. Various frolics similar to those practised in Europe among older people, were at this period carefully licensed in New York, and the exceeding capacity of Von Donderdonk's person indicated an equal capacity to endure a jest. On the 1st of April, 1771, this gentleman, as usual, took his seat in a commercial coffee-house, and was presently accosted by several of his class and acquaintance. When he moved homewards, they all followed, and till a great crowd of gazers assembled, he was not aware how strangely he was attended by a procession of at least forty persons all nearly of the same rotundity. Finding they had all been collected by cards of invitation to dine with him, he had the good nature and good sense enough to give them a very friendly dinner impromptu; but the contrivers of this scene took pains to report that Von Donderdonk held on this day at his house a mysterious meeting of Cabalists whose persons were enlarged by bladders of air, bags of earth, and tubes of gas, according to Rosicrucian art. Now though it was pretty certain that neither air nor water had much share in the elements of his large company's composition, Donderdonk was not free from general suspicion of a tendency to occult science. He was very fond of believing that the Freemasonry cultivated in New York was a branch of that secret school which amused and frightened Europe more than six centuries. And as he was clearly convinced that the disciples of Paracelsus and Hermes had made great advances towards the great discovery of transmuting certain metals into gold, his love of gelt stimulated his zeal for science.

There was then in New York a sort of supernumerary or factitious lodge of Freemasons, who affected, under the seal of most profound secrecy, to initiate novices into the true Eleusinian mysteries of their craft without the preludes and delays of elder brethren. This whimsical fraternity held occult correspondence with a man in high office, whose frugal habit of carrying his negro boy behind him on the same horse gave great offence to decorous magistrates, and food for much conjecture to Mynheer Donderdonk, who conceived this personage's black page must be no less than such an imp as the great Cabalist Paracelsus kept in his sword's pommel. This idea redoubled his zeal to be one of the initiated among the Free Brothers. After much ceremony and many bribes his wish was granted; but whether he learned the art of building arches without a keystone, which ancient masons are said to have made the true secret of their brotherhood, or whether he was taught the sublimer art of changing himself into any element he pleased, like a Rosicrucian, will never now be known. But it is certain that his personal circumference was reduced at least one half, and seemed composed of much lighter particles; and the mere sound of a Freemason's symbol in a workman's hand, or the sight of their mystic triangle, made his face peak itself into at least as many acute points. But he nursed in his mind such a spirit of revenge as Dutchmen are famed for shewing; and as the little lean personage who rode with his black page *en croupe* had been the chief cause of his initiation, he singled him out as the subject of his slow and silent vengeance.

The separation of America from her mother-country caused the dispersion of nearly all the special lodge of Free Brothers,[1]

---

1 This merry fraternity of college-youths was well known to the gallant and amiable General H-m-lt-n, to John J—, afterwards President of the Congress, and his cousin the Bishop-elect of New York, of whom as McFingall, the American Hudibras, says, "Next V—d—ll, that poetic zealot, / I see a lawn-bedizen'd prelate."

and the grand master was supposed to have migrated to the continent of Europe, where various vicissitudes conducted him at last as a bookseller to Berlin. But his taste and skill in literature, and a spirit of research which poverty could not suppress, gave him a kind of fame among the itinerant collectors and Jew-brokers frequent at continental fairs. By one of these far-dealing travellers his name was brought to the ear of his ancient enemy, who gave such instructions to his Prussian correspondent as he thought likely to ripen his plan of retaliation. This correspondent was a banker of some note, acquainted with many state-secrets, the keys of which are usually of gold or steel. He was the agent of a fraternity said to be Freemasons, but in reality a knot of literary conspirators, aiding and aided by those daring wits and politicians whose axes were then laid at the root of ancient governments. They were in quest of a credulous enthusiast fit to act a part in a necromantic farce designed to dupe one of their patrons. Von Donderdonk represented the quondam Freemason as a most convenient tool, and his friend the banker described him to the Secret Society accordingly.

In the dead hour of a cold midnight Schimelpenink, as the American brother now called himself, was seized at the entrance of his obscure lane, blindfolded and carried through sundry winding streets and passages till a sharp fresh air informed him he was in some large or uninclosed space. A loosening purposely permitted in the bandage over his eyes allowed him to see several muffled figures passing and repassing in such attire as might grace an Auto-da-fé. A hollow voice very near his ear began by asking if he had repented all his sins, or how many remained to repent. Famine and persecution had wrought hardly on the poor American's nerves, and he bethought himself with some remorse of the mummeries he had practised under the sacred symbol of Freemasonry. His joints slackened, and his hair, if age had spared any, might. have realized the tale of Mr. Ledupe's, which a single night made grey. The familiars who seemed to know and resent the impositions he had practised in their semblance, deposited him in a stone sarcophagus, desiring him to commune with his conscience and prepare himself to learn those cabalistic secrets he had mimicked and profaned. Now though a frightened man has seldom any curiosity, he is apt to be very conscientious; and two hours confinement in cold and darkness added to hunger, created all the terrors the Secret

Society could desire. Two of their servitors raised him from the stone cistern, covered with the dews of agony, and commanded him to ascend the ladder of three thousand steps by which the Illuminati ascend into the presence of that omniscient eye selected for their symbol from Hindoo mythology. Supported by these two, and in the utmost tribulation of spirit, poor Schimelpenink toiled up his endless ascent, tottering, trembling, and beseeching the merciful care of his guides. The buz of voices which had sounded close to his ear at first, became gradually fainter till it seemed lost in distance; and the thin sharp air which met his face announced his approach to the intense cold of the upper regions. His terror and convulsive shiverings became too intolerable for mortal strength to bear or see; and a sudden burst of hideous sounds, which appeared to his strained fancy like the cackle of demons, but was in part only an explosion of uncontroulable laughter, from many mouths, so harrowed his nerves that a he fell from his dizzy height over the two stools which formed the ladder in a deep swoon. "This fellow will do for us," said the cabalist whose office had been to place the stools alternately under the feet of their dupe. "He will need neither syrup of borage, nor John of Munster's lectures to make him mad. Let our Electro-magus make ready his magic lantern, and he will see and say what we please when our other novice arrives to be instructed."

This charitable philosopher immediately called for his comrade's assistance, and deposited our American in a sack for further use, in a dry corner of an outer chamber ventilated by a large grate in the wall. The air or the motion of the sack, for it was not too rigidly tied, had just begun to recall Schimelpenink's breath, and his mind was in a frightful dream of demons and inquisitors, when his eyes opened and beheld a little lean man dressed exactly like himself, looking into the mouth of the sack. The frightened scholar began a prayer in a curious mixture of Saxon, Arabic, and modern Greek, till his apparition interrupted him. "Mutter no exorcisms to me—I am thy good genius. Creep out of that grate and into thy garret silently like a true American Musquash, and let me get into thy sack." Schimelpenink climbed more like a wild cat than the dull animal his visitor named, and was out of sight in the twinkling of an eye. The new occupier of the sack rolled himself up in the least compass possible and remained quite still in his corner till the servitor of the Secret Society took him on his back and thrust him into the cavity of a closet from whence he heard the muttered dialogue of the familiars.

"Will he not shrink, think you?"

"There is no fear—he is a thorough believer in Hermetic craft, and as our banker tells me, has the rarest dreams we could devise when his head is properly stirred."

"But if our patron should insist on questioning him?"

"Let him answer for himself—he has heard strange things and will say he has seen the Millennium. Could you not see how his imagination travelled when he thought himself going up the ladder, and you blew the great bellows in his face?"

The agent of the Cabalists could not forbear a fit of laughing—"Well, I have some curiosity myself to know what account he will give of the upper regions which he was so afraid to stay in. Let us take him out of his corner and give him a little celestial refreshment." The sack was accordingly placed upright on a table, the muffled head allowed to come forth above it, and a few ambrosial pastilles burned near the nose. This ceremony over, the sack was again drawn loosely up, and a voice made powerful by a large silver tube, spoke from the lower part of the academic hall.

"Where hast thou been?"

"In the air," replied the occupier of the sack in a tremulous voice.

"What hast thou seen there?"

"All that are hanging, all that may, and all that *shall* be hanged."

This reply rather startled the examiner, but he consulted his formula and proceeded.

"What sawest thou upon earth?"

"The foolish, the half-wise, and the all-wise."

"Who are they?"

"The foolish are the women of this world—the half-wise are their husbands, and the all-wise is I myself." There was another buz at this reply, but it expressed approbation, and the clerk of the society resumed his questions. "If thou art all-wise, thou knowest what the King of Prussia does at this moment?"

"He is thinking of an ugly, lean, ungrateful, Frenchman, with a hawk's nose, a viper's eye, and a tongue like a salamander, for it dwells in nothing but heart-burning. The rogue has made himself the King's confidante, and the King intends to make him his old clothes' merchant and patcher of loose shreds."

A pause of silence was broken by a shrill voice asking—"What sawest thou in Geneva?"—The sack replied—"A mad man writing letters to posterity, which the postmaster-general Time will never deliver. Moreover, he is preaching humanity, but leaving his children to the Foundling Hospital; and striving to educate men as if nature had not made fools enough. But he has some good in him for he hates Voltaire."

"What will the King of Prussia say to the Calvinistic curate who has asked preferment at Neufchatel?"—"'Tarry at Jericho till thy beard is grown:' and he will give the same answer to young philosophers."

"Ask him," said a whispering female voice, "what the witty, the beautiful, and the celebrated Madame De——d is now saying to the minister of the Bavarian court?" As if the ears of the oracle in the sack had been sharpened by blindfolding his eyes, the instant answer was—"They are saying nothing—the lady sits with her feet on the fender—the gentleman with his eyes on his snuff-box, both yawning at their ease. Because they were ridiculous forty years ago in each other's company, they think it their duty to be dull no where else now."

"If thou hast seen all things," resumed the inquisitor in a more solemn tone, "thou hast seen our brothers in France. What do they to-night?"

"They are quarrelling over the blue bib of the little Dauphin,[1] and his cousin of Orleans swears it shall be a crimson one ere long. A cup of brandy given to a drunken courier, saved Monk's head, and restored Charles of England: a scarlet feather placed in a coquettish woman's cap, cost Peter of Russia his crown and determined his vixen-wife to be an empress: an affront to a printer in green spectacles lost America to England; and a courtezan's lock of yellow hair may split the alliance of the Illuminated. They are debating now whether Monsieur Neckar's daughter or himself ought to be prime-minister."

"How will the debate end?"

The voice changed slightly and replied in a low and deep tone—"None present here will see!—There are men of high souls and women of rare beauty holding council to-night on the fate of Europe—it will be with them in twenty years as it will be with all that inhabit this world in a century. Of all that exist now upon this earth when the hundredth anniversary returns, only a few helpless wretches will remain—but of that divan before the twentieth

---

1 The cordon bleu was put on the late Dauphin in the cradle.

year is past, there will be but one!—I shall not live to tell you this again."[1]

A profound and long silence followed, and the secret council looked upon each other with conscious dismay and a deeper feeling of superstitious awe in themselves than they had hoped to create in others. Presently there was considerable hurry and commotion as if some great drama was rehearsing, and the muffled prisoner was suddenly placed near, a crevice in a dark curtain and desired to tell what he discerned through it. There was a slight shivering in his envelope and he muttered to himself *"Dans peu de temps je te rápprochera!"* Then replacing instantly the bandage over his face, he said to the audience—"I see the shadow of a woman whom a misjudged father sacrificed, forgetting that generous men never cease to love what is pesecuted:—and I see a likeness of a thoughtless boy who pleased his Prince by calling himself his faithful Diaphané, and had not wit enough to escape the gallows by forsaking him. I also see a blue-eyed man who would have been unhappy if they had not died, for he might not else have had the pleasure of believing two

---

1   Laharpe records a similar prophecy. All Europe knows how well it has been verified.

people loved him."—"Who is that blue-eyed man?" was asked by many voices. The orator in the sack replied, "He is a prince who loves war and snuff, and hates women as much as the gallant Prince de Condé feared the sound of his mistress's high shoe-heels, after she had wounded him with his own sword which she mistook for a long turkey's feather. He has kept Voltaire to tickle and keep him awake, but begins to think a hair from any other old fox would do as well. He gave D'Alembert a snuff-box because it was too little for a king after a fop had dipped his fingers in it. He laughs to see Rousseau making himself and the editor of the St. James's Chronicle believe that Frederic the Great is afraid of him. As if it was any shame to be libelled by a man who would slander his Creator *if he knew him!*"

"Thou hast not yet answered our former question fully;" rejoined the agent of the assembly in a raised tone—"What employs the King of Prussia on this day?"

"This morning," replied the invisible speaker, "he was conjugating the verb Ennui at Sans-souci—I am tired, thou art tired, he is tired, &c.—this evening, he has devised a new amusement and has ordered his serjeant-major to give a hundred lashes each to about forty gentlemen who are meddling in what does not concern them." As he spoke, he dropped the bandage, the sack, and the threadbare coat that covered his favourite uniform, and they saw Frederic the Great himself. His blue eye had something paralyzing in it, for those who might have attempted escape stood stupidly gazing while the serjeant of the guards entered to execute their sentence. It was fulfilled with great impartiality, upon the spot in the presence of the King, who dismissed the cabalists very good humouredly after their flagellation, saying he had given them *another secret* to keep.

IV

ON the evening of the 29th of June 1555, in one of the narrow streets near the Poultry Compter in London, a dark square-built ruffian, in a thrum cap and leathern jerkin, suddenly sprung forth from his hiding-place, and struck his dagger with all his force against the breast of a man passing by. "By my holidam," said the man, "that would have craved no thanks if my coat-hardy had been thinner—but thou shalt have a jape[1] for thy leman to know thee by"—and flourishing a short gisarme, or double-pointed weapon, in his left hand, with his right, on which he seemed to wear an iron glove, he stamped a sufficient mark on the assassin's face, and vanished in a moment.

"Why, thou Lozel!" said another ruffian, starting from beneath a penthouse, "wast

1 A fool's mark.

playing at barley-break with a wooden knife? Thou wilt hardly earn twenty pounds this bout."

"A plague on his cloak, Coniers!—he must have had a gambason under it—Thou mayest earn the coin thyself—thou hast gotten a gold ring and twenty shillings in part payment."

"Get thee gone to thy needle and baudekin again, like a woman's tailor as thou art! Thou hast struck a wrong man, and he has taken away thy nose that he may swear to the right one—That last quart of huffcap made froth of thy brains."

"My basilard is sharp enough for thee, I warrant"—muttered his disappointed companion, as he drew his tough hyke or cloak over his bruises, and slunk into a darker alley. Meanwhile, the subject of their discourse and of their villainy strode with increased haste towards the Compter-prison, and enquired for the condemned prisoner John Bradford. The keeper knew Bishop Gardiner's secretary, and admitted him without hesitation, hoping that he brought terms of grace to the pious man, whose meek demeanour in the prison had won love from all about him. The Secretary found him on his knees, as his custom was, eating his spare meal in that humble posture, and meditating with his hat drawn over his face. He rose to receive his visitor, and his tall slender person, held gracefully erect, aided a countenance which derived from a faint bloom and a beard of rich brown, an expression of youthful beauty such as a painter would not have deemed unworthy the great giver of the creed for which he suffered.[1] Gardiner's secretary uncovered his head, and, bending it humbly, kissed his hand with tears.

"Be of good comfort, brother," said Bradford—"I have done nothing in this realm except in godly quietness, unless at Paul's Cross, where I bestirred myself to save him who is now Bishop of Bath, when his rash scrimon provoked the multitude."

"Ah, Bradford Bradford!" replied his visitor, "thou didst save him who will burn thee. Had it not been for thee, I had run him through with my sword that day!"—Bradford started back, and looked earnestly—"I know thy voice now—and I remember that voice said those same words in my ear when the turmoil was at Paul's Cross.—For what comest thou now? a man of blood is no fit company for a sinner going to die."

"Not while I live, my most dear tutor—I am Rufford of Edlesburgh."

---

1 Some account of this extraordinary man may be found in Middleton's *Biographia Evangelica*.

The old man threw his arms round his neck, and hung on it for an instant—"It is twelve years since I saw thee, and my heart grieved when I heard a voice like thine in the fierce riot at Paul's Cross—Art thou here bodily, or do I only dream?—There is rumour abroad, that thy old enemy Coniers slew thee at Huntingdon last year."

"He meant well, John Bradford, but I had a thick quilted pourpoint and a tough leathern cap—I have met his minions more than once, and they know what print my hand leaves. Enough of this—I am not in England now as Giles Rufford; I shall do thee better service as what I seem."

"Seeming never was good service," said the divine—"what hast thou to do with me, who am in God's hand?"

"He makes medicines of asps and vipers," answered his pupil—"I shall serve him if I save his minister, though it be by subtlety. I have crept into Gardiner's favour by my skill in strange tongues and Hebrew secrets, therefore I am now his secretary: and I have an ally in the very chamber of our queen-mistress."

"That woman is not unwise or unmerciful," replied Bradford, "in things that touch not her faith; but I will be helped by no unfair practice on her. Mercy with God's mercy will be welcome, but I am readier to die than to be his forsworn servant."

"Master, there can be no evil in gathering the fruit Providence has ripened for us. Gardiner was Wolsey's disciple once, and hath more heathen learning in him than catholic zeal. There is a leaven left of his old studies which will work us good. He believes in the cabalism[1] of the Jews, and reads strange books from Padua and Antwerp, which tell him of lucky and unlucky days. He shall be made to think to-morrow full of evil omens, and his superstition shall shake his cruelty."

"Thou art but a green youth still," rejoined Bradford, "if thou knowest not that cruelty is superstition's child. Take heed that his heathenish witchcraft doth not shake both thy wit and thy safety. For though I sleep but little, and have few dreams of earthly things, there came, as I think, a vision raised by no holy art, into my prison last night. And it had such a touch of heaven's beauty in its face, and such rare music in its voice, that it well nigh tempted me to believe its promise. But I remembered my frailty, and was safe."

---

1 Raimond Lully derives this word from the Arabic, and interprets it "superabundant science." His commentator Cornelius Agrippa goes great lengths into it.

The Secretary's eyes shone brightly, and half a smile opened his lips. But he lowered both his eyes and voice as he replied, "What did this fair vision promise?"

"Safety and release, if I would trust her, and be pledged to obey her."—There was a long pause before the young man spoke again— "Do you not remember, my foster-father, the wild laurel tree that grew near my birth-place? An astrologer at Pisa told me it should not wither till the day of my death—And it seems to me, when I have walked under its shade, that the leaves made strange music, as if a spirit had touched them. It is greener and richer than its neighbours, and the fountain that flows near its root has, as men believe, a rare power of healing—the dreams that visit me when I sleep near it are always the visitings of a courteous and lovely spirit—What if the legends of Greece and Syria speak truth? May we not both have guardian spirits that choose earthly shapes?"

"My son," replied Bradford, "these thoughts are the diamond-drops that lie on the young roses of life—But the Sun of Truth and Reason should disperse them. Man has one guardian, and he needs no more unless he forgets that One. Thou wast called in thy youth the silken pleader, because thy words were like soft threads spun into a rich tissue. Be wary lest they entangle thee, and become a snare instead of a banner fit to guide Christians.—I am a blighted tree marked for the fire, and thou can'st not save me by searing the freshness of thy young laurel for my sake."

"I will shame the astrologer tomorrow," said his pupil; "and therefore I must make this hour brief. She who rules the Queen's secrets has had a bribe to make Mary merciful. There is hope of a birth at court, and death ought not to be busy. Fare-ye-well!—but do not distrust that fair apparition if it should open these prison-doors to-morrow."—So saying, the young man departed without heeding Bradford's monitory gesture.

Stephen Gardiner, Bishop of Winchester and High Chancellor by Queen Mary's favour, sat that night alone and thoughtful in his closet. He had been the chief commissioner appointed to preside at Bradford's trial; and though he had eagerly urged his colleagues to condemn him, he secretly abhorred the timeserving cruelty of Bishop Bonner and the cowardice of Bourne, who had not dared to save the life of the benefactor he had once begged to save his own. "You have tarried late," said Gardiner, as his secretary entered—"the stars are waning and their intelligence will be imperfect."

"I traced it before midnight," replied the Secretary, "but I needed the help of your lordship's science."

"It is strange," said his patron, leaning thoughtfully on one of Roger Bacon's volumes, "that men in every age and climate, and of every creed, have this appetite for an useless knowledge—and it would be stranger, if both profane and sacred history did not shew us that such knowledge hath been sometimes granted, though in vain.—What is that paper in thy hand?"

"It is a clumsy calculation, my lord, of this night's aspect. I learned in Araby, as your lordship knows, some small guesses at Chaldean astrology; but I deem the characters and engraved signs of the Hermetic Men[1] more powerful in arresting the intelligent bodies in the heavens. They were the symbols used by Pythagoras and Zoroaster, and their great master Apollonius."

"Ignatius Loyola and Athanasius Kircher did not disdain them," replied the Bishop,

---

1 Hermes Trismegistus, founder of this sect in Egypt, is said to have lived in the year 2076, in the reign of Ninus after Moses. The Rosicrucians, a similar sect, appeared in Germany in the beginning of the seventeenth century, calling themselves the enlightened, immortal, and invisible.

crossing himself—"But what was the fruit of thy calculation?"

"Nothing," answered his Secretary, humbly—"nothing, at least, not already known to one abler than myself. The first of July is a day of evil omen, and the last day of June has a doubtful influence. My intelligence says, if life is taken on that day, a mitre will be among ashes."

"Ha!—and the heretics will think it if Bradford dies—for they are wont to say, he is worthier of a bishopric than we of a parish-priesthood.—Thou hast not yet told all."

"My lord, I see the rest dimly.—There are symbols of a falling star and a flame quenched with blood. They tell of a gorgeous funeral soon."

Gardiner was silent several minutes before he raised his head. "Thou knowest, Ravenstone, that I was, like the Jesuit Loyola, a student of earthly things, and a servant in profane wars, before I took the cross. Therefore I sinned not when I learned as he did. And thou knowest he thought much of heathen and Egyptian conjuration—But that is not my secret. Plato and Socrates had their attendant demons—I have seen, it may be, such a one in a dream last night. Methought there stood by me in my oratory a woman of queen-like stature and strange beauty. She shewed me, as it were beyond a mist, a green tree growing near a fountain, and the star that shone on that fountain was the brightest in the sky: but presently the tree grew wide and broad, and the light of the star set behind it. Then I saw in my cathedral at Winchester mine own effigies on a tomb, but all the inscription was effaced and broken except the date, and I read 'the first day of July.'—Is it not strange, Ravenstone, that a dream should so well tally with thy planetary reckoning? Yet I was once told by a witch-woman, that the Bishop of Winchester should preach our Queen Mary's funeral-sermon."

"So he may, my lord," said the Secretary, who called himself Ravenstone—"but there may be a White Bishop of Winchester."

"Ah! I trow thy meaning—White is a shrewd churchman, and looks for my place. Hearken to me, then—I have a thought that evil is gathering against me to-night;—to profit by my dream, I will go privily from London within this hour, and abide in secret at Winchester till the ides of June are past. But take thou my signet-ring, and put my seal and countersign to Bradford's death-warrant when it comes from court."

"Does my lord think it will be sent?" said the Secretary, calmly—"They say the Queen's bed-chamber-woman has told her, she will be the mother of no living thing if she harms ought that has life."

"Tush—that woman is a crafty giglet, but we need such helps when a queen reigns. It was well done, Ravenstone, to promise her Giles Rufford's lands. Since the man is dead, and his heir murdered him, we will make Alice of Huntingdon his heiress."

Not a muscle in the pretended Ravenstone's face changed, and his deep black eye was steady as he replied—"It will be well done, my lord, if she is faithful. At what hour is John Bradford to die?"

"Bid the marshal of the prison have a care of him till four o'clock to-morrow, for he is a gay and glorious talker—and so was his name-sake, mad John[1] of Munster, even among red hot irons. Look to the warrant, Ravenstone, and see it speedily sent to Newgate. That done—nay, come nearer—I would speak in thine ear. There is a coffer in my private chamber which I have left unlocked. Attach my signet-ring to the silver chain, and let me know what thou shalt hear:—but let this be

1 John of Leyden, a butcher, and afterwards a furious mistagogue, was cruelly executed at Munster, in 1533.

done in the very noon of night, when no eye or ear but thine own can reach it."

Ravenstone promised, and his hand trembled with joy as he received the ring. It was already almost midnight, and Gardiner, as he stole out of his house, stopped to look at the moon's rainbow, then deemed a rare and awful omen. "Alice of Huntingdon is busy," he said, with a ghastly smile—"but the dead man's land will be fee enough for the blue-eyed witch—she cannot buy a husband without it."—And stealing a look at Ravenstone, the Chancellor-bishop departed.

"I am a fool," said Ravenstone to himself, "and worse than a fool, to heed how this wanton giglet may be made fit for a knave's bribe, and yet that this dull bigot, this surly and selfish drone, should have such glimpses of a poet's paradise, is a wonder worth envying. I have heard and seen men in love with Platonic superstition under the hot skies of Spain, where the air seems as if it was the breathing of kind spirits and the waters are bright enough for their dwelling—but here!—in this foggy island—in this old man's dark head and iron heart!—I will see what familiar demon stoops to hold converse with such a sorcerer." And young Ravenstone locked himself in his chamber, not ill-pleased that his better purpose would serve as covert and gilding for his secret passion to pry into his patron's mystery. He arrayed his person in the apparel he had provided to equip him as Gardiner's representative; and while he threw it over the close pourpoint and tunic which fitted his comely figure, he smiled in scorn as he remembered the ugliness and decrepitude he meant to counterfeit. At the eleventh hour, when the darkness of the narrow streets, interrupted only by a few lanterns swinging above his head, made his passage safe, he admitted himself into the Bishop's house by the private postern, of which he kept a master-key. By the same key's help he entered the chamber, and ringing his patron's silver bell, gave notice to the page in waiting that his presence was needful. When this confidential servant entered, he was not surprised to see, as he supposed, the Bishop seated behind his leathern screen muffled in his huge rochet or lawn garment, as if he had privately returned from council, according to his custom. "Hath no messenger arrived from the court?" said the counterfeit Prelate.—"None, my lord, for the Queen, they say, is sore sick."—"Tarry not an instant if one cometh, and see that the Marshal of the Compter be waiting here to take my warrant, and execute it at his peril before day-break."

The page retired; and Ravenstone, now alone, saw the coffer standing on its solitary pedestal near him. It was unlocked, and he found within it only a deep silver bowl with a chain poised exactly in its centre. Ravenstone was no stranger to the mode of divination practised with such instruments.[1] What could he risk by suspending the signet-ring as Gardiner had requested? His curiosity prevailed, and the ring when attached to the silver chain vibrated of itself, and struck the sides of the bowl three times distinctly. He listened eagerly to its clear and deep sound, expecting some response, and when he looked up, Alice of Huntingdon stood by his side.

This woman had a queen-like stature, to which the height of her volupure, or veil, twisted in large white folds like an Asiatic turban, gave increased majesty. Her supertunic, of a thick stuff, in those days called Stammel, hung from her shoulders with that ample flow which distinguishes the drapery of a Dian in ancient sculpture. "You summoned me," she said, "and I attend you."

Ravenstone, though he believed himself sporting with the superstition of Gardiner

---

1 A follower of Roger Bacon practised this mode, and pretended the ring would give such answers as the celebrated Brazen Head. "Time is, time was, time past," &c.

as with a tool, felt startled by her sudden appearance; and a thrill of the same superstitious awe he had mocked in his patron, passed through his own blood. But he recollected his purpose and his disguise; and still keeping the cowering attitude which befitted the bishop, he replied, "Where is thy skill in divination if thou knowest not what I need!"

"I have studied thy ruling planet," said Alice of Huntingdon, "and as thy wishes are without number, so they are without a place in thy destiny. But I have read the signs of Mary Tudor's, and I know which of her high officers will lose his staff this night."

"Knowest thou the marks of his visage, Alice?" asked the counterfeit Bishop, bending down his head, and drawing his hood still farther over it.

"Hear them," replied Alice: "a swarthy colour, hanging look, frowning brows, eyes an inch within his head, hooked nose, wide nostrils, ever snuffing the wind, a sparrow-mouth, great hands, long talons rather than nails on his feet, which make him shuffle in his gait as in his actions—these are the marks of his visage and his shape—none can tell his wit, for it has all shapes.—Dost thou know this portrait, my Lord of Winchester?"

"Full well, woman," answered Ravenstone, "and his trust is in a witch whose blue eyes shame heaven for lending its colour to hypocrisy; and her flattery has made boys think the tree she loved and the fountain she smiled on became holy. And now she serves two masters, one blinded by his folly, the other by his age."

Ravenstone, as he spoke, dropped the rochet-hood from his shoulders, and shaking back his long jet-black hair, stood before her in the firmness and grace of his youthful figure. Alice did not shrink or recede a step. She laughed, but it was a laugh so musical, and aided by a glance of such sweet mirth, that Ravenstone relaxed the stern grasp he had laid upon her mantle. "The warrant, Alice!—it is midnight, and the marshal waits—where is the warrant for John Bradford's release?"

"It is in my hand," she said, "and needs only thy sign and seal—here is the handwriting of our Queen."

Ravenstone snatched the parchment, but did not rashly sign without unfolding it—"Thou art deceived, Alice, or willing to deceive—this is a marriage-contract, investing thee with the lands of Giles Rufford as thy dowry."

"And to whom," asked she, smiling, "does my queen-mistress licence me to give it by her own manual sign?"

Ravenstone looked again, and saw his own name entered, and himself described as the husband chosen for her maid of honour by Queen Mary. "Has she also signed," he said, "the reprieve of John Bradford?"

"It is in my hand, and now in thy sight, Henry Ravenstone; but the seal that will save thy friend may not be placed till thou hast given sign and seal to this contract. Choose!—"

The warrant for Bradford's liberation was spread before him, and her other hand held the contract of espousals. He smiled as he met the gaze of her keen blue eyes, and wrote the name of Henry Ravenstone, in the blank left for it. She added her own without removing those keen eyes from his; and placing the parchment in her gipsire, suffered him to take the warrant of his friend's release. It was full and clear, but when he turned to seek the Chancellor's signet-ring, the coffer had closed upon it. "Blame thyself, Ravenstone!" said Alice of Huntingdon—"thou hast laughed at the tales of imps and fairies, yet thou hadst woman's weakness enough to pry into that coffer and expect a miracle. As if thy master had not wit sufficient to devise a safe place for his ring, which thy curiosity placed there more than thy obedience! Didst thou think I came into this chamber like a sylph or an elfin, without hearing the stroke on the silver bowl which gave notice thou wast here!—Truly, Ravenstone, man's vanity is the only witch that governs him."

"Beautiful demon! when the crafty churchman who tutors thy cunning has no need of it, will thy other master, the great Prince of Fire, save thee from the stake?"

"My trust is in *myself*," she answered; and throwing her cloak and wimple on the ground, she loosened her bright hair till it fell to her feet, waving round her uncovered shoulders, and amongst the thin blue silk that clunk to her shape, like wreaths of gold. Her eyes, large and brilliant as the wild leopard's, shone with such imperial beauty as almost to create the triumph they demanded. "Be no rebel to my power, Ravenstone, for it is thy safety. Gardiner has ordered Bradford's death without appeal, and feigned his dream of danger to decoy thee here! But I have earned a fair estate by serving him, and thou mayest share it with me."

"Thy wages are not yet paid, Alice!" he replied, grinding his teeth—"That fair estate is mine, and that contract can avail thee nothing without my will—Henry Ravenstone is a name as false as thy promise to save Bradford."—Alice paused an instant, then laughing shrilly, clapped her hands thrice. In that instant the chamber was filled with armed men, who surrounded and struck down their victim notwithstanding his desperate defence. "This is not the Bishop!" one of the men exclaimed—"this is not Stephen of Winchester—we shall not be paid for this."—"He is Giles Rufford of Huntingdon," answered his companion, the ruffian Coniers—"and I am already paid."—Alice would have escaped had not the length of her dishevelled hair enabled her treacherous accomplices to seize it. They twined it round her throat to stifle her cries, making her boasted beauty the instrument of her destruction.[1] She was dragged to Newgate on a charge of sorcery, and executed the next morning by John Bradford's side in male attire, lest her rare loveliness should excite compassion. He knew her, and looking at the laurel-stems mingled with the faggots, said, as if conscious of his young friend's death—"Alas! the green tree has perished for my sake!"—It was indeed his favourite laurel, which had been hewn

1 Coniers and his gang confessed their guilt before the Queen's Council in November 1555.

down with cruel malice for this purpose. The people, just even in their superstitions to a good man's memory, still believe the earth remains parched and barren where John Bradford perished on the first of July 1555; and his heart, which escaped the flames, like his fellow-martyr's, Archbishop Cranmer's, was embalmed and wrapped in laurel-leaves. His memory is sanctified by the religion he honoured—while Alice of Huntingdon's sunk among dust and ashes, as a worthy emblem of the Cabalism she practised.

V

THERE appeared at Spa, in the year 1720, a young gentleman, whose fine figure and good equipage created what is now called a great sensation. He had all the wit and learning of that day; talked to the ladies of the plurality of worlds in the style of a junior Fontenelle, and quoted Montesquieu to the gentlemen. He dropped one day from his pocket an extract from Voiture's correspondence which furnished half the *petit-maitres* of Spa with pretty billets during the season. Then he affected great knowledge of state-mysteries: shook his head when Prince Eugene was named; hinted at Queen Anne's love for her brother, and said something strange about the French lady whose accouchement took place in King James's palace, and was foster-mother to his heir-apparent. As there is remarkable sympathy between similar characters, the Chevalier

Valamour, as he chose to call himself, became very intimate with an obscure watchmaker in the suburbs of Aix-la-Chapelle. If this recluse had been the Emperor Charles V. in his watchmaking frolic, he could not have known more of men and manners. He had also a surprising familiarity with the names of learned physicians, and now and then dropped mystic phrases of cabalistical import. He had a daughter whom he secreted in a corner of his miserable house, and guarded with the most anxious care. Our Chevalier was duly fascinated with her beauty, and took all the pains required in the beginning of the eighteenth century to recommend himself. Not that he fully understood his own meaning, for he had a most religious horror of a woman's tongue, especially a wife's. Linnæus himself, whom he partly resembled in genius, was not more unfortunate in a shrewish mother than he had been. His father's lady had compelled him to sweep his own room, prepare his own breakfast, and perhaps to hem his cambric ruffles. Certainly this woman's violence of power had contributed to excite and fix his imagination on the idea of a placid beauty as the most perfect. And as he probably did not find one exactly realized in the common world, he read romances, and especially the "Count de

Gabalis," till he conceived something of the kind might be found elsewhere. Ariette was more like the charming creature detained in the palace of silence by the King of the Fishes than any human female he had ever seen. She seemed to have chosen Madame Dacier's motto, "Silence is the ornament of women;" if indeed she had a choice, which certain mysterious motions of the father's head rendered doubtful. One thing was remarkable:—he could never prevail on her to shew herself by moonlight, nor to lift her veil when he had spoken to her half an hour. At the expiration of that time she always dropped the light and elegant screen of black silk net which was constantly attached to her fine hair. This, and the marble paleness of Ariette's countenance, gave something of poetic sanctity to her character, which her profound modesty and secluded mode of life completed. He was often tempted to propose himself to the ancient watchmaker as a son-in-law, but his reverence for him as a man of science was not quite enough to subdue the pride of birth, and some hereditary fears of a wife's dominion. At length fear and pride gave ground, and the chevalier made a suitable speech in the artist's study. To his great surprise, the offer was rejected, but with an air more in sorrow than in anger.

He repeated it, and was promised a month's consideration. Before the end of that time, he was informed the watchmaker had suffered an apoplectic stroke, and lay at the point of death. He ran to him—the old man was expiring, and had only strength to put a small ring on his finger before he breathed his last. The room was silent—there was no spectator but himself, and a crowd of alembics, phials, and chemical preparations, lay in one corner. The suspicion he had always entertained that the deceased artist studied alchymy, and had probably discovered the long-sought secret of creating gold, induced our chevalier to search into the heap under which rested a little iron box. He soon perceived that the ring put on his finger by the dying man was contrived to act as a key, and it readily unlocked the coffer. There were in it only a few mysterious calculations, and one on which a horoscope was constructed. Underneath it, in Romaic characters, he decyphered words to this import.

"My art informs me you will find this parchment on which your nativity is accurately traced. Ariette is not of my nature, nor have I power to bestow her. What her veil conceals I never knew, nor can I recollect any change in her aspect, though she has dwelt here many years; but I am at no loss to guess her purpose.

Sylphs, gnomes, nymphs, and salamanders, are incapable of enjoying eternity, unless by marriage with a Christian. They have then the power of sharing earthly happiness, and their partners, if they choose, may share with them that intellectual soul which is the spirit of eternal life. Or if they so please, these husbands may content themselves with their society during the short period which the order of their nature permits them to exist in human shape—Ariette is, as I humbly guess, a sylph or spirit of the purest element. For she has no interest in the world's wealth, no delight in its tumults, no capacity for ardent, jealous, or hostile feelings. She thinks, she acts, and she speaks, by the rule of reason;—but——"

The manuscript broke off, as if a sudden sickness had arrested the writer's hand. To whom this could be addressed, unless to him, was not to be conjectured, and Valamour went home in great agitation. The very few neighbours who had seen Ariette, celebrated her domestic virtues, her charities, and unimpeachable prudence, during her residence of ten years' length among them. He could judge for himself of her grace and beauty: what could he risque by marrying her? If the Romaic manuscript was a fable, it could no way harm him—if it stated truths, it increased his chance of happiness. Valamour's heart was better than his head;—it prevailed, and he married Ariette.

On his marriage-day, the bride's conduct gave some countenance to the dead cabalist's assertion. For instead of the grateful tenderness which might have been expected to touch an orphan raised from poverty to a noble rank, Ariette shewed a reserved, calm, and gentle demeanour, which expressed more good-sense than sensibility. Valamour, however, was delighted with his prospect of escaping all the turmoils caused by an impatient spirit, and enjoying perpetual serenity with a wife altogether *reasonable*. On the third day after their nuptials, the Chevalier conducted her to a carriage without saying a word of its destination, which she never enquired, and the next morning brought them to a charming villa in the midst of a rich Provençal valley. It was late in spring, but few flowers had made their appearance, except in a little recess near the Garonne, where a perfect bower of roses was spread. "These," said he, "are all the offspring of a sprig planted by my mother, who won in her youth the Crown of Roses given as a trophy of merit by the owner of the Chateau de Salency. You must have heard of that affecting ceremony, and I hold these

rose-trees as the best part of my patrimony."
—"There is no *reason* for it," she answered
coldly:—"these roses are no way conscious of
their origin, nor a part of your mother's merit—if they were, you have no right to it—If,
indeed, they had been reared and nursed for
you by your grateful peasants, like the roses
of M. de Malesherbes, you would have *reason*
to be pleased with them."—Valamour was
piqued at this reply, and obliquely reproached
her with a want of that feeling which in such
cases is more delightful than reason.—"It is
not my fault," she returned, with the same
coldness—"it would be as wise to quarrel
with these flowers because they have not the
waving branches of the willow, as to be angry
with me because I cannot feel like you. And if
you are angry, that is no reason why I should
be displeased with you, because you do not
feel that you are unreasonable."—Valamour
was highly displeased; but after recollecting
himself awhile, he began to consider that his
anger was useless, and might be absurd. If her
supposed father's words were true, Ariette had
no power to understand his feelings unless he
could infuse into her that human and tender
spirit which her nature had denied her. There
was something pleasant to his vanity in believing that this fair creature depended on him, as

the cabalist said, for the gift of a soul, and for the length of her existence. He returned into her presence, determined to excuse the defects of her imperfect frame, and to remedy them if he could by kindness.

These defects were by no means so easy to endure as he had expected. The eternal level on which an ill-natured fairy condemned her victim to walk for thirty years under an unchanging blue sky, was an Eden compared to the dead calm of Ariette's temper. And the most provoking part of this calmness was, that it shewed itself most when he was in a rage. If he hunted and returned in all the glee of a successful sportsman, she wanted to know the reason of his delight. If his friends or vassals fêted, or congratulated him, she analyzed their compliments, and could not find them reasonable. If he brought her a bouquet, or a gallant madrigal on her beauty, she laid the one aside as useless, and burned the other when she had read it, "because," said she, "that is all that can be done with it." What a mortification for a poet! Valamour actually looked again into the cabalist's fragment, to read the words which hinted she could not live for ever.

It would have been well for Valamour, however, if all his wit had been as little regarded. But certain persons at Aix-la-Chapelle had paid more attention to his jeux-d'esprit, and some rumours of the sagacious guesses he had made on political matters found their way to Versailles. The consequence was, a domiciliary visit to search for treasonous papers; seals of office were put on the doors of his villa, and a mandate was presented to him, requiring his attendance at the Secretary of State's bureau under an Exempt's escort. He never doubted the willing attendance of his wife, and was confounded at her refusal. "There can be no use in my stay with you in prison," she said, "therefore you ought not to be so unreasonable as to require it."—"What, madam! you feel no necessity to prove your duty and attachment to me?"—"None at all, monsieur, unless you can prove that I have failed in either. I should only add to your distresses in Paris, and you to mine—I may be as well employed here, and shall stay, where I am."—"There wanted only this to convince me the cabalist spoke truth," said the angry husband, and departed alone, satisfied that she neither had a soul, nor ever could have one: and he comforted himself again by remembering her term was short.

Our Chevalier was accused of having asserted, that the celebrated prisoner in the Iron Mask was the last-born twin-brother of

Louis XIV. and his impertinent conjecture was punished by a confiscation of his estate and a decree of banishment. Permission, however, was granted him to sell the furniture and heir-looms of his patrimonial villa, and to visit it for ten days without official superintendence. He returned to the Provençal valley in extreme ill-humour; and much as he had been chagrined by his wife's coldness, he was glad to find some one forced to listen to his tale of grievances. She heard the sentence of exile and deprivation with admirable fortitude, but her husband would have been more pleased if she had raved at his enemies and deplored her ill-fortune. He wanted a pretext to scold and lament, and was angry that she seemed wiser than himself. He walked out to his favourite recess in the valley, and found the sacred rosebushes torn up by the roots, the gates of his gardens broken, and all the outrages of petty and vulgar malice committed by the peasantry, now no longer his vassals.—"And why," said Ariette, who walked by his side, "are you heart-struck by this?—Of what use to you were these men's acts of false servility, and what harm is there in their open hatred? Let them shew it as often as they will by such acts—they are only ills because you think them such—Feel them no longer, and you disappoint your enemies. They have had more trouble in pulling up these paltry thickets of roses than you had reason to value them."—"But my mother!—was it nothing to see a memorial of her goodness?—I need it, madam, I assure you, to prevent me from growing ferocious."—"Very well, chevalier! and if you had no better reason for your goodness than the sight of a few rosebuds growing where your mother's died twenty years ago, your ferocity will be more honest and more natural."

Valamour's fury rose beyond his power of self-command, and he uttered all the bitter upbraidings his wit could devise; for anger and despair are oftener witty than love. They lasted half an hour without provoking a single retort from Ariette; but as her watch, on which she looked with vexatious calmness, indicated the thirtieth minute, she dropped her veil, and turned to leave him. This act recalled to his mind the custom she had religiously observed before her marriage—he had never held her in passionate discourse so long after, and it cooled his emotion by reminding him of the strange circumstances connected with her character. While he hesitated and thought of snatching off the mysterious veil, she retired in silence, sighing deeply.—"How intolerable is all this meekness!" said poor Valamour to himself—"If she would be angry sometimes, I could be angry myself at my ease."

At the supper-hour he found her sitting alone near a table, dressed with the graceful order of happier times. They were to depart to-morrow; and this parlour—this hearth which his childhood had endeared to him, the portrait of his father, the grave of both his parents seen in the soft moonlight, recalled all that was kind and good in Valamour's temper. Ariette lifted up her veil, and seated herself at the head of the table, lighted only by the beams of the summer-moon. It touched her countenance with singular beauty, not rendered less affecting to her husband's eye by novelty, for this was the first time she had ever permitted herself to be seen by him in the moon's light.—"To-night," she began, breaking a long silence, "is the anniversary of our marriage, and the seventeenth since—but it is not yet time to speak of that.—You were displeased with me for paying but little attention to the rose-trees you respected—I planted another during your absence at Paris, and these are its first productions—perhaps they will not displease you, for *they must die to-night.*" And smiling sorrowfully, but with great sweetness, she placed on the centre of the table a basket of white roses, and retired.—Valamour was surprised and touched by her last words, and still more when, by drawing out a branch of the flowers, he discovered a large quantity of gold coin and several jewels beneath them. A leaf of ivory in a corner of the basket offered itself next to his notice, but the words pencilled on it made him forget every other part of the gift.

"You have often asked me why I refused before our marriage to be seen by you in the moon's light. A follower of the Cabalist's Red Cross would tell you that souls are aptest to be communicated in her presence, therefore I declined the hazard *then*—and since our marriage you have not seemed disposed to give me any part of yours.—A veil must cover the remainder of my few days, for you have not wished to prolong them: but though I cannot give you life, I leave you the means of living nobly till your term is ended."

Valamour made but one step to his wife's apartment, and found it vacant. He was, as all perplexed men are, extremely angry that he had not foreseen this event. Then he wondered at his own ill-temper and impatience; and though he had almost begun to hate his wife, was heartily chagrined at her sudden and final departure; for with all her provoking calmness, she had been a convenient and patient subject of complaints and murmurs, when it suited him, as it sometimes suits every man, to find a passage for his spleen. In a few hours, all that was beautiful and uncommon in Ariette came thronging on his fancy: the last words of her letter began to alarm him, and he looked at his horoscope once more. By long and anxious references to the astrological books of her reputed father, he had discovered signs and combinations which informed him that his line of life was threatened on the day that deprived him of his wife. Our chevalier became dull, dejected, and sickened as if he had eaten of the Obi-poison. In two or three months he was pronounced in a confirmed decline, and the best physicians attended him in vain. One of great eminence at Aix-la-Chapelle offered his services, and came with due ceremony into the sick man's room. When alone with him, he said, "If you were a common hypochondriac, Valamour, I would force you to laugh by compounding certain medicines in your presence, and inducing those grave men, your other physicians, to taste them. But I shall try plain truth. Who am I?"

"Erasmus Haller, a most learned and benevolent practitioner—the friend of sick and dying men."

"I am also, or I was, the friend of your dead father-in-law, and have some interest in the French court, which I have used to obtain a revocation of your sentence. This is my first medicine—my next is, to translate your horoscope truly. He who drew it was a sufficient cabalist, for he knew human nature wants no help from other elements. He saw you had been made afraid of ordinary women by a fierce stepmother, and tempted to look for extraordinary ones by old romances. So he devised this scheme of your nativity to ensure a good husband for his daughter. He told you, *if* she was a sylph or spirit, she had but a short term of certain life, and he thought,—how true and beautiful was that thought!—that you could not fail to treat her gently while you remembered she might die in another moment. Who could be harsh or unjust to another, if that remembrance was always present, as it ought, to all of us?—He thought her quiet character would suit yours, and perhaps be animated by it, as he chose to hint in a poetic way, which gave you, no doubt, much comfort and encouragement. At least, like a wise father, he ensured your care of her by knitting your line of life with hers. Come, forgive the cabalism, and be content with a mere woman, composed, as all the sex are, of both sylph and salamander. If she refused to go with you to Paris, it was because she could serve you better by coming to beg my help, and by selling her jewels to buy the court's pardon. And now she comes to beg, not to buy, yours."

Ariette came in covered with her veil, and stood at a timid distance, though beckoned forwards.

"Do you not see," said the good physician, "the moon is waning, and this is the moment when a gentle soul may be communicated!"

"I give her mine fully and for ever," said her husband, "if she drops that mysterious and cabalistic veil."

"Ah!" she replied, "be prepared to see me with a different face—I wore it only when I felt my aspect changing to one which might displease you."—and after a little pause she threw off her veil, and discovered eyes full of laughing brightness, and cheeks which betrayed, notwithstanding the tears that still glistened on them, a few dimples ready to express some merry malice.

"Be a shrew sometimes, but a tender-hearted woman always!" said Valamour, throwing the horoscope into the fire; and Ariette, who never wore the veil again except when his peevishness required her silence, preserved no other secret of cabalism.

VI

IN the month of August, 1798, a vessel
steering towards the western entrance of
the straits of Magellan was stranded on a
reef of coral rocks, and went to pieces. One
Frenchman swam on shore, accompanied by
a Gentoo servant, whose efforts saved him
from perishing. The Island on which chance
had cast them appeared not more than a mile
broad, crossed by a deep valley. In the centre
of this valley, surrounded by a thick planta-
tion of bananas and plantain trees, the two
shipwrecked strangers found three rows of
houses, each in the form of an oblong square,
with a shelving roof, supported by seven posts
on each side and three in the middle. The
eaves reached within two feet of the ground,
leaving the rest open and unwalled. These
roofs or eaves were composed of palm-leaves,
thatched with a degree of skill and symme-

try that promised civilized inhabitants. The Frenchman took a branch of the Mimosa tree, knowing how generally its tender and flexible leaves are respected, perhaps because they seem even to rude nations an emblem of courtesy, and presented himself at the first hut's entrance. He was surprised to receive a courteous answer from a gentle voice in the English language. The speaker had the features of a Briton, though shaded with a deep olive tint; and the white cloth which covered his tall and well-shaped figure was arranged in something like European costume. The stranger spake English well, and was instantly surrounded by all the residents of this valley, hailing with cries and gestures of joy, the countryman of their ancestors. Their welcome was shared by his Gentoo attendant, who knelt humbly to receive it, and both were led into the central hut, seated on a bench covered with soft matting, and feasted on delicious fish. Delombre was cautious to avail himself of fortunate accidents, and spoke of England with the glee and familiarity of a native. He heard the traditions of the islanders, who informed him, that an accident very similar to his own had thrown an English ship on what they called the coast of Omorea, about the year 1649. The passengers in this crew were a person named Digby, his family, and a few of his friends, emigrating to the new southern world from the turmoils of rebellion. These had been the parents and founders of the colony, in which Delombre was surprised to find no traces of Christianity. There was, indeed, a Moravian regularity in the movements of the whole. The central hut was so contrived as to command a view of those that surrounded it, and they, resting on detached pillars of the clustered stems of trees, formed a perspective on all sides not unlike the arcades of the Banian tree. The inhabitant of this centre was invested with the office of chief magistrate, and teacher of those mysteries which seemed to be at once their law and gospel. At first Delombre was cautiously and reluctantly admitted among the audience, but his profound and submissive attention gained their confidence. He then discovered, that the seven props of every house alluded symbolically to the seven metals, the seven planets, and the seven days' work of creation: that they believed in two things, a good, and an evil spirit, and expected a millennium or perfect state of man at the end of a thousand years. In preparation for this great sabbath, they appeared to live in an entire community of brotherhood and peace. Their huts or dwellings were all equal; the little isle was common property, like lands of ancient parishes; and their boats were divided into small allotments of the same size, in which, whatever was the success of any individual in fish, he was only permitted to deposit as much as it would contain, and to distribute the rest among his companions. On the same principle, the public granary was subject to the equal demands of every family, and the cloth which their mulberry trees' bark afforded belonged not to the manufacturers, but to the commonwealth. Punishments seemed hardly needed, for the mild temperament of these people, subdued by a pure and moderate diet, incessant labour, and the total absence of all excitements to love, avarice, ambition, or revenge, almost promised to realize their hope of perfectibility. Love was no passion here, for the young women of the island, seen all day at work in their open huts in the plain clothing never permitted to be embellished, had none of the charms afforded by seclusion, mystery, or parade. The mayor, or chief magistrate, united them in the central pavilion of the valley, and dissolved their contract when they complained of discontent, which seldom happened, for neither party could gain any thing by a change, except a new progeny, and a consequent increase of labour. There was no ceremony, no congratulations, no change of scene or dress, to flatter the imagination; and love, as Rochefoucault merrily says, was never known, because it was never spoken of.

Delombre, a pupil of Rochefoucault in manners, but of a much deeper philosophy in other points, was surprised and strongly interested by this Utopian island. He easily perceived in the obscure creed of its inhabitants the relics of that superstition which prevailed among the Rosicrucian[1] or Hermetic men, the Cabalists, Platonists, and Illuminati of the Dutch and German schools in the sixteenth century. He remembered the name of Digby among their disciples, and had no doubt that the father of this colony was some kinsman of the Sir Kenelm Digby, famous for his faith in the dreams of Jacob Behmen, and John of Munster during the first Charles's reign. He was surprised to find such a community of men governed by the simple levelling principle of those enthusiasts, without any help from the more solemn inventions and witcheries of Dr. Dee, and Hugh Peters. He rather expected to have found in this relic of

1 Some account of these dreamers may be found in D'Argenson, and Burton's *Anatomy of Melancholy*. The 574th. No. of the *Spectator* alludes to them with poetical complacency.

their sect some traces of the beryl glass and magic tripod by which those impostors either duped or aided the reformers of Cromwell's days. And he was not mistaken. For on the seventh sabbath after his arrival in the island, he witnessed an assembly of the eldest men held in silence at midnight, "under the close shade of innumerous boughs," while their chief read from the remnant of a very ancient bible certain strange, and dark texts in the Apocrypha. And there was a rude altar of stone on which a plate[1] of some mixed metal was fastened, inscribed with Egyptian characters, and covered with a crimson veil, which none but the patriarch presumed to raise. "I am not mistaken," said Delombre to himself: "the vision of universal equality and perfection, and the omnipotence of God and Matter, or rather of Matter without God, has found its way from the Magians recorded by Plutarch, through the secret tribunals of Westphalia, the elegant academies of Descartes and Spinosa, and the roundheaded, crop-eared dupes of

---

1 Perhaps something similar to the round plate usually attached to the Abacus, or staff of office, carried by the Knights-Templars, who are supposed to have learned the original mysteries of Cabalism in the early days of Crusading, and to have diffused them on their return from the East.

an English parliament's hired wizards, to this paradise in the Southern Seas!—Plato himself, who expected that golden period when 'all mankind should be one family, having all things in common and one form of speech,' would have yawned if he had spent seven weeks in the dullness of this 'equal republic of the elect.'—I marvel that the Rosicrucian Digby did not enrich his colony with a few sylphs and nymphs exempt from the domestic drudgery of this levelling system, and bring the Houris of the Manichean heresy into his island-tabernacle, though he could not find the elixir of life or the seed of gold. Let us see whether we cannot enliven the dull matter which composes these people with some finer touch of the *fifth element* they expect."

Delombre began by recommending himself to his new friend's esteem by the urbanity and gentleness of his conduct. He assisted his Gentoo servant in constructing several ingenious toys and utensils in addition to many they possessed, especially a flageolet and a guitar capable of great sweetness. He observed that all their domestic articles were constructed of bone very neatly polished, or of wood, but never of metal, and he concluded that their creed forbade its use, as the founder of Digby's philosophy taught the depreciation of all metals. Delombre's ardent spirit seized on this opportunity to realize or establish the full extent of the Rosicrucian creed, to try its influence over a simple race of men, and to see its consequences. The inhabitants of this isle, whose very name had some reference to the Chaldean root of Rosicrucianism, seemed formed for his disciples; and their isle, perhaps, might be the first theatre of a cabalist's dominion. Delombre's meditations were interrupted by the person who held in this island an office nearly similar to the patriarch of St. Kilda's. When they had walked together a few paces—"This," said he, "is the place where by burying our dead we restore them to the basest of the four elements mystically mingled in us. Look round and tell me what you see."

"I see," replied Delombre, "a sandy plain, without tree, stone, or beacon. The darkness that lies beyond passes my sight."

"You are right," said the Patriarch, "and such is the state we live in here. There is a dry smooth level crust spread over the corruption at work beneath. Our wretched people lie under the weight of our barbarous equality, a prey to vile paltry passions, ever grovelling and coiling, as the dead lie under this soil devoured by earthworms—yet the quietness

103

of the grave appears outside!—Here is neither flower nor tablet to honour the dead, nor have the living here either joy or honour. All is blank, barren, and dark, yet this burial-place is better than our life, for our life is a death we feel."

Delombre's brow became black, and he cast a fearful glance towards the dark cavern which terminated the prospect.

"None but the dead are near us," continued the Patriarch, "and we may speak safely of what concerns the living. You cannot desire to remain here—Assist me in completing the boat I have secretly begun to build, and we may escape together."

"From hence," said Delombre, in surprise—"from this quiet and free island—to navigate an unknown sea, and visit strangers?"

"Yours," answered his companion, "was not the first vessel that has touched it; but what you have told me is enough. I loathe the poverty, the sameness, the torpor of our existence here. Where men build towers and cities and palaces, they must have property and hope. They would not plough, nor reap those rich fields you tell of, nor come forth in such gallant vessels, if there was no better prize for their labour than the pittance given to all men. If they have churches, they must feel or know something of a GOD. England, they say, has all these—Men are not buried there like dogs, nor born only to eat, sleep, and die—Here, we have nothing else to do."

"What!" said Delombre, contemptuously—"to see a few useless palaces and churches, would you leave the bones of your fathers, the young men born under your roof, and the mother who reared them?"

"I tell you," the Patriarch answered, "we have no property and no hope. Our iron law gives all things alike to all men—the idle, the witless, the gormandizing, and the ungrateful. Our women are dull as the wood which kindles our fires—What more are they to us, or we to them?—Our children owe us nothing, for we cannot enrich them—they are sure of bread and sleep whether they are the drones, or the bees of this hive. The drones may devour their morsel of honey, and the most industrious bees have no better share. Therefore we heed them and they heed us no more than the swamp regards the water it sucks in and never yields again. We are like the rushes in a swamp—equal, it is true, but all feeble, and soon withered.—In England—"

"In England," interrupted the Frenchman, bitterly, "the commonwealth is a tree which they are hewing down because the roots cannot be at the top, and every branch cannot bear at once both blossom and fruit. There is not a pool in your island sooner disturbed by a pebble—not a bunch of dry fern on your hearths more easily kindled into a blaze than the owners of those broad fields and rich cities!—Nor is there a nook in the most savage corner of the world which they are not readier to dwell in than their own!"

"But they may *hope!*" exclaimed the Patriarch, his dark eyes gleaming and expanding—"they may range—they may rave—they may mistake evil for good, but there is a good in view, and if they fall sometimes, they are free to rise. They are not forced to live in the deadness and desert of an eternal Level.—Their tree bears fruit, and every man may strive to reach it. Friend!—my night's prayer and my morning dream is to see that land, where there is a race to run, and a prize to win."

"And I," said Delombre, "have spent my manhood in flying from such vanities. I once believed some childish tales, but I have shaken them off—and instead of hoping for an hundred ages beyond the grave, I enjoy the present."

"You believed and hoped this once!" rejoined the Patriarch, stopping short, "and you strive to forget it? I would give all the years of my past life for one day of such belief. Well—thou may'st teach it me, however; and I will make these senseless grovellers happy before I go. They look for a change into some unknown element a thousand years hence—let us give them a nearer and better hope."

The philosopher smiled in scorn, and promised to instruct him in those cabalistic secrets which govern and amuse men.

Delombre, however, had no intention to amuse his new acquaintance with the whims of cabalism respecting the mighty secret of generating gold, or its pretended parent mercury.[1] Neither did he suppose that such a secret, even if he had possessed it, would have been more useful to him, than to its owner Paracelsus, who died ridiculously poor, notwithstanding the help of his gold seed, and the imp he kept in the pommel of his sword: both as unprofitable as the mice he pretended to make out of meal. But he erected in the hut allotted to him certain machines calculated to excite the curiosity of the people; and with great mystery informed their Patriarch that he belonged himself to the creed of their English

1 The alchymists Von Helmont and Fludd pretend that mercury is the original principle of gold, and sulphur of the inferior metals. And they affect to suppose them typically represented by Adam and Eve.

Ancestor. "But," said he, "you are aware that he did not live long enough here to convey to his descendants the inmost secret of his faith. That which you obscurely call the Creator of the world, is the substance that fills it. Since all things, even the impalpable air, is material—that is, a mass of matter—the power that sways all things is in it, and matter itself is the divinity."

There was darkness in this light, and the old man he addressed only trembled and was silent. But when the younger men of the community gathered round the orator, he took care to clothe his mystery in gayer colours. He told his hearers, that the air, the fire, the water, and the earth which they beheld, were inhabited by particles endued with life like themselves, but too delicate to be discerned by common eyes. "Their business," he added, "is to watch, to assist, and to bless us. They are unacquainted with the toils and afflictions of bodily existence—their beauty is unchanging, their power is pleasure, their presence is the highest gift of science. They are always near. Even while we speak they hear us now, and their exquisite voices are prevented from reaching us only by the dullness of our own composition."

These hints and disclosures were not given at the same time, nor without the aid of such pageantry as his situation afforded. He shewed them at a certain hour, after much awful preparation, the concave mirrors in a globe of glass by which the fire of the sun could be concentrated, and a powder obtained capable of the most marvellous effects. Another glass, filled with water, earth, and air, was placed mysteriously on a kind of altar exposed to the sun; and these three elements, he said, would soon be separated and reduced by his art to a medicine sufficient to prevent all want of food and drink. If the natives could have paused in the simplicity of their ignorance, before they credited his assertions, his eagle eye, the authority of his noble brow, and the powerful music of his voice, would have enforced belief; and the charm of a romance so new and rich wanted little more than its own influence.

The evening of that day had more than the usual softness of a southern clime. But the natives of Omorea did not retire as usual to sleep after their contented labours. Many remained couched under the fragrant trees, watching the stars as they came forth in their beauty, and listening to the murmur of waters in which they already imagined whispering voices. The next day did not restore the quiet regularity of their routine. They met in groupes, to talk, to wonder, and to regret that these invisible creatures of light and loveliness were not made known to them. They surrounded Delombre's dwelling, and demanded his assistance. He told them their obedience must be strict and their patience determined. They answered by shouts of joy, and by bearing him in triumph on a litter of palm-branches to the chief-place or centre of their city, installing him as their priest and king. The deposed patriarch retired gloomily with a sullen gesture. His broad firm neck and the tiger-profile of his iron-countenance gave no indication of the yielding temper manifested by his companions. Delombre graciously dismissed his new subjects, and closing all the entrances of his sanctuary, began his preparations. But an eye not wholly ungifted with the craft of cabalism was upon him.

Within one month he had promised to provide that mercurial elixir by which the spirits of other elements would be rendered visible. He believed himself very well able to delude their expectations by the magic of chemical flames and vapours, and by farther promises couched in such mysterious jargon as would feed their appetite for wonders. Indistinct hopes of novelty and change were, as he well knew, the moving springs by which men govern others; and he smiled as he planned the revolution he expected to complete in this little empire. The Gentoo slave who had accompanied Delombre in his voyage from the Indies, had been one of the first subjects of his experimental cabalism. He had found this man in the diamond mine of Sultan Saib, and obtained him as a gift from his owner. The profound ignorance in which Azim had lived till his nineteenth year, the meekness of his temperament, the idolatrous gratitude he shewed for his redemption, made him ready to receive, as Delombre believed, whatever creed he offered. He was therefore, in some measure, a being of his own creation. During the voyage that followed Azim's removal from the darkness of the mine, he could learn but little of earthly things, and his master's powerful genius enslaved him again. Delombre hoped and studied to preserve this uncultivated Gentoo in utter ignorance of all pure religion and all law, and to make him what he chose to call a man of nature. It was necessary, however, to retain his services; and these he thought himself able to command by the force of gratitude, and the awe his mysterious actions imposed. For Azim knew that Delombre had brought a box of diamonds from the wreck, and had saved other treasures. He also knew that his master visited a secret place in the island unknown to its natives, and there held conferences with a creature whose like he had never seen. He had been told that this creature, invisible to all others, was the Spirit of fire that obeyed Delombre, and preserved him from every evil chance. So much his master had chosen to assert, for he knew the power of mystery over the ignorant, and he felt, though he did not confess to himself, that a servant bound by no moral law, must be bound by fear. He was right in his feeling—wrong in his expedient. Fear had not power enough to suppress the growth of envy in Azim's mind. He knew the diamonds were precious, and his master's caution had not sufficed to prevent him from discovering the place of their concealment, nor his frequent interviews with that nameless spirit, which, like the Peris of his own clime, might, as he supposed, be gracious to the love of a true Gentoo. This thought dwelled on his mind in solitude and silence till the night when Delombre's eloquence gained him the Patriarch's place. His sullen and melancholy eye caught the deposed Patriarch's as he retired in anger, and they met in the thick woods near the shore. Azim shewed him the secret cavity in a rock near a well of brilliant water; over-hung by the broad leaves of a bread-fruit tree. The moon whose last quarter was to mark the period fixed for fulfilling Delombre's promises, was now waning fast: but her light in a sky thick set with stars sufficed to shew his enemies their way into his sanctuary. It was a recess, a chamber scooped in the sand-rock, illuminated only by a silver glimmering of the sky seen through a fissure in the loose stone that guarded its entrance, and by a burning pine-branch within. The Patriarch ventured near enough to look in, and saw Delombre sitting on a mat at the feet of what might well seem an ethereal spirit. There was a transparent and bloodless fairness in the face, a shadowy uncertainty in the outline of the figure, and a fixture in the large blue eye that seemed of no earthly mould. And Delombre's attitude and movements were those of a supplicant eagerly and devoutly bending before an idol.—"It is too late!" answered a voice whose very sound was suited to the spirit of beauty—"Your success, Delombre, will be your bane. Why were you not content with their amity and hospitable shelter? You have been ungrateful, and your craft will teach them cruelty."

"How have I deceived them?" said the Frenchman, starting up—"The cabalistic fool who brought this colony here spoke in parables, but he felt truths. He felt as I feel, that every man has in him a fiery nature, if a kindred spark can be found to rouse it, though it may be encumbered with cold and earthy dross. And though I could not raise a spirit as Lilly[1] and Booker did, aye, and their own sorcerer Dee, I could have shewn these English islanders a rarer apparition than they ever dreamed of, if you would have been induced to aid me. They believe only Azim and myself escaped from the wreck—they cannot know you to be an Englishwoman and my fellow-passenger. Only represent for a few moments the friendly spirit of fire, as for your sake I provoked a worse element."

"I could not assist you," replied the melodious voice, "to act imposture always with success. You have already disturbed the quiet of these harmless natives by a fable, and the wildness of unreasonable hopes will end in revenge.—You saved me from the sea where I was perishing—you have fed and sheltered me in this strange land—save me for a better purpose than mockery and profanation."

---

1 William Lilly was astrologer to the English parliament in 1648. The exorcist Kelly is said to have conjured up dead men at Halifax and Lancaster, and in the presence of Alasco, King of Poland; and his successor, Dr. Dee, amused King James I. in the same way.

"Should I have dared," interrupted Delombre, advancing still nearer, "to have mocked these islanders by shewing them a prize I never meant to part with? Or is it profanation to shew it as if it was indeed something of divinity beyond their reach—No, Aglae; it does not need the solar powder of the cabalists, nor their doses of water, earth, or air, to exalt the fire within us, or to make the baser elements prevail over it. They said truly that light was the soul of all things; for when the Creator sent light, he sent Beauty into the world, and I act under its influence."

"Delombre!" said the voice, in a shriller tone, "Thou hast spoken a word that assures me I am safe—Thou hast named thy Creator, who has formed nothing without some touch of good, therefore I will not fear though there is now no light except his presence."

At that instant the stone barrier of the cave was forced back, and the Patriarch entered. Delombre felt all his peril, and the depth of his errors. He uttered a desperate oath of vengeance on his betrayer, and strove to seize the Patriarch's throat. "Save that woman and yourself," said the islander, calmly; "your slave has sold your life. I learned once to be a Christian, and have not forgotten what I learnt."—Delombre fixed a ghastly and suspicious glance upon him. The islander only replied, "*God sees us!*" and put his axe into the Frenchman's hand. In another instant the cave was filled with armed men guided by Azim. The unclouded moon shewed him their weapons, but the same moon shewed them the beautiful shadow of a woman, standing as if hovering on a raised point of the rocks. While Delombre clove his treacherous slave's head with one stroke of his axe, the Patriarch trampled on the burning pine-branch, hoping to prevent the aim of the assassins. He was too late. An arrow whistled through the cavern, followed by a yell echoed on every side. All the islanders were assembled in the madness of excited rage, threatening, scoffing, and demanding his promised art. Aglae seized the half-extinguished pine-branch, and threw it among the heap of dry leaves and flowers collected for her couch. The pile sent up a column of fire, above which she appeared standing like the spirit of the element. Her outspread arms and pale countenance, gleaming in their deathly whiteness through its crimson volumes, struck the slaves of an unholy superstition with awe. They fled, uttering dismal shrieks, and a pause of silence and darkness followed. Aglae descended to her lover's side. "Their boat is moored in the creek, Delombre, and they are far off!—Seize it, and escape while they still fear the fire-spirit—The continent is not distant, and we can but die."—She gave into his hands the chest of diamonds and a basket of the bread-fruit, but the Patriarch caught her in his arms, and ran to the creek, where his boat lay provisioned for a fishing-voyage. He had scarcely pushed it from the shore before the shouts and clang of the armed islanders were heard behind them. Well-managed oars and a rapid current carried them soon beyond reach, but the flash of fire-brands and the whizzing of arrows shewed the fierce spirit of their enemies. "Such are men, then," said Delombre, "without a GOD!"—He looked towards Aglae, but her frozen eye made him no answer. He raised her head—her long hair was stiff and matted, and lifting it from her throat, he saw the broken point of an arrow fixed in it. "They were not deceived," she said, smiling in her last agony—"I have an immortal spirit!"—"I believe it *now*," he answered,—"and its creator must be a Divinity."

A PARTIAL LIST OF SNUGGLY BOOKS

ETHEL ARCHER *The Hieroglyph*
G. ALBERT AURIER *Elsewhere and Other Stories*
CHARLES BARBARA *My Lunatic Asylum*
S. HEZOLNRY BERTHOUD *Misanthropic Tales*
LÉON BLOY *The Tarantulas' Parlor and Other Unkind Tales*
ÉLÉMIR BOURGES *The Twilight of the Gods*
CYRIEL BUYSSE *The Aunts*
JAMES CHAMPAGNE *Harlem Smoke*
FÉLICIEN CHAMPSAUR *The Latin Orgy*
BRENDAN CONNELL *Metrophilias*
BRENDAN CONNELL *Unofficial History of Pi Wei*
BRENDAN CONNELL (editor)
     The Zinzolin Book of Occult fiction
RAFAELA CONTRERAS *The Turquoise Ring and Other Stories*
DANIEL CORRICK (editor)
     Ghosts and Robbers: An Anthology of German Gothic Fiction
ADOLFO COUVE *When I Think of My Missing Head*
QUENTIN S. CRISP *Aiaigasa*
LUCIE DELARUE-MARDRUS *The Last Siren and Other Stories*
LADY DILKE *The Outcast Spirit and Other Stories*
CATHERINE DOUSTEYSSIER-KHOZE
     The Beauty of the Death Cap
ÉDOUARD DUJARDIN *Hauntings*
BERIT ELLINGSEN *Now We Can See the Moon*
ERCKMANN-CHATRIAN *A Malediction*
ALPHONSE ESQUIROS *The Enchanted Castle*
ENRIQUE GÓMEZ CARRILLO *Sentimental Stories*
DELPHI FABRICE *Flowers of Ether*
DELPHI FABRICE *The Red Sorcerer*
DELPHI FABRICE *The Red Spider*
BENJAMIN GASTINEAU *The Reign of Satan*
EDMOND AND JULES DE GONCOURT *Manette Salomon*
REMY DE GOURMONT *From a Faraway Land*
REMY DE GOURMONT *Morose Vignettes*
GUIDO GOZZANO *Alcina and Other Stories*
GUSTAVE GUICHES *The Modesty of Sodom*
EDWARD HERON-ALLEN *The Complete Shorter Fiction*
EDWARD HERON-ALLEN *Three Ghost-Written Novels*